ISS Stargraber

Nicolas Pollet

Dedication

This novel is dedicated to my wife, who encouraged me over the years to bring my imagination to life.

About the Author

Nicolas Pollet is a 56-year-old man living in Geneva, Switzerland. He is a multidisciplinary artist whose main passions reside in Photography, music and writing. His love for Sci-Fi and action-packed movies from his youth led him to write this novel. His mantra as a novelist is "read the action, see the action."

Prelude

Silence at last The Bugatti Veyron reached 192 miles per hour. Nevertheless, John Desmond and his wife, Isabella, chatted calmly about the evening they had just spent at the Blue Moon Café.

John, a former Navy fighter pilot, had a pronounced taste for speed in all its forms, with one exception: the sanitised speed of today's flycars. He preferred those classic vehicles where man and machine were one.

"Pat and Robert got on my nerves again tonight," Isabella gushed.

"Yes," John replied, concentrating on the road ahead. "You know how they are. The very idea of staying alive on Earth upsets them to no end."

"Still," John added, "they know our position on the matter, but they always have to insist."

"You know," she said, looking up at the sky through the panoramic glass roof of the Bugatti, "even though I helped build that thing up there, I'll never set foot in it."

"I know, sweetheart, but you're not going to change them any time soon. You have to accept them as they are. They're good friends."

Isabella gave John an amused look.

"You're too kind, my dear, which is probably why I love you so much."

John replied with a movement of his eyebrows that only he knew the meaning of, signifying that his love for her was matched only by her beauty. It had indeed been ten years since John and Isabella met at a Navy party thrown by Isabella's father, General Moore, for the retirement of veterans of the Factional War. They married six months after falling in love at first sight.

Accustomed to the uniform, Isabella had quite literally melted when she saw her father present John with the Purple Art for bravery in battle. At six feet tall and 80 pounds of muscle, he exuded a quiet strength that was reassuring at first glance.

John, on the other hand, was more difficult to destabilise. A loner with a big heart, he had never committed to a lasting relationship. He was probably afraid of hurting the one he loved if something happened to him during his dangerous missions. But he would never admit it to himself. Isabella, a woman of great beauty and subtle intelligence, quickly realised that the best way to win John's heart was to appeal to his undying admiration for her father.

So, she arranged for her father's general to invite John to her ranch in the Canadian Rockies for a weekend of rafting.

From that famous weekend on, they never left each other's side, and their love grew by leaps and bounds. Not unlike John's Bugatti, still speeding along Highway 66 at over 190 miles per hour.

Only 30 miles away was the southern exit to the megalopolis of Albuquerque. John and Isabella lived on a ranch high above the upscale neighbourhoods of Santa Fe. Albuquerque had become a megalopolis after the Big One of 2112. The entire west coast of the United States had gone under in less than an hour. Ten million dead—for a catastrophe that experts at the time linked to Mayan predictions of the end of the world a hundred years earlier. The survivors of San Angeles were driven inland, and Albuquerque quickly became the new megalopolis of the West Coast.

John was about to catch up with a Type 1 Flycar, so he stepped on the accelerator.

"John, please," said Isabella. "You know I don't like you driving too fast."

"Yes, sorry," replied John, who always had a good excuse for stepping on the gas.

"But it's Archi's flying car, honey," John insisted. "Since he's a manual pilot, if I don't pass him before the exit, I'll have to fight him all the way home. You know, I love the teacher, but he drives like an iron on oilcloth."

"Be careful," Isabella insisted.

Flycars were hovering vehicles powered by liquid hydrogen engines. They were fully automated. The first generation 'A-Types' offered autopilot only on main roads, and their speed was limited to 186 miles per hour. That was more than enough excuse for John to let the 16 cylinders of his vintage Bugatti rumble.

199, 205, 217, 236, 253 miles per hour—foot to the floor—John honked the horn as he passed the professor's flying car.

Crazy driver, thought Professor Mac Dugan as he recognised the Desmonds' car. Archi Mac Dugan was an expert in orbital physics. He was undoubtedly the family's best friend.

"Slow down, John, this is our exit," said Isabella calmly, used to her husband's antics.

"Slowly," she repeated in a more energetic tone.

John's eyes hardened in an instant.

"What's wrong?" Isabella asked, worried.

"I don't know," John stammered. "I've got a problem. I can't brake, nothing responds. The steering wheel—I can't steer…"

"Careful!" cried Isabella.

At that speed, in manual gear, the freeway exit came at them like a bullet. Despite his sharp reflexes, John—no longer in control of his vehicle—was unable to avoid the guardrail between the freeway and the exit. Knowing what lay ahead, he had just enough time to grab Isabella's hand and give her one last look of love.

In a split second, the guardrail propelled the Bugatti 164 feet into the air. Like a ground-to-ground missile, the car crashed through a self-illuminating LED road sign. The explosion of the sign resembled a fireworks display, each of the thousands of self-powered LEDs flickering in a gigantic spray as the vehicle passed through.

Frozen with the fear of seeing herself die, Isabella immediately lost consciousness. John, accustomed to the most extreme situations, waited anxiously for his car to land.

Wait, this is going to hurt my John, he thought.

The extra 492 feet the car travelled before crashing felt like an eternity. His only thoughts were of Isabella. They had to get out of this—both of them. They loved each other too much not to.

The car plunged down now, coming inexorably closer to the ground. John instinctively tightened his grip on Isabella's hand.

And then—contact with the ground. Brutal.

In a thousandth of a second, under the force of the impact, all of the car's airbags deployed. John was still conscious. One, two, five, then six rolls… By the end of the tenth, John lost count. The Bugatti's windows had all exploded in a deafening crash. With a final jolt, the car finally stopped spinning like a figure skater at the Olympics.

Before blacking out, John glanced at the speedometer, which was stuck at 227 miles per hour.

My God, what have I done?

Her eyelids, burning with the blood that covered them, closed.

Finally, silence at last.

Chapter One
The End of His Certainties

On the morning of 10 June 2153, three years after his terrible accident on Highway 66, John Desmond was not the same man.

The loss of his wife, Isabella, had hit him hard. He felt responsible for the terrible drama that had unfolded that night.

John lay on his bed. A soft, soothing voice said, "It's 7:30, John. Time to wake up. You've got a big day ahead of you."

"Damn alarm clock," he muttered.

John was still drunk from the previous day's excesses, as he had been all too often for nearly three years. Everything was jumbled in his head. He didn't even know where he was. Every time he woke up, it was the same ritual: rousing himself from a restless sleep and realising that he still missed Isabella. Then he had to regain his human face in less than an hour so he could get on with his day's work.

8 a.m. John finally awoke from his half-sleep, got up and, as he did every morning, made his way to one of the glass walls of his

bedroom, as if to get a better sense of where he was. It was dark outside, and the stars shone with a rare intensity.

This sky is as black as ever, he thought. He knew exactly where he was now—on the Stargraber Geo Orbital Station.

At the end of the 20th century, several nations joined forces to create the International Space Station (ISS). Designed for scientific research in space, by the end of 2011 it consisted of some fifteen pressurised modules joined together to form what was then the largest man-made object in Earth orbit.

One hundred years later, just before the Big One—the dreaded earthquake that had always threatened the megalopolis of San Angeles—the ISS had become the Stargraber Geo Orbital Station. More than a thousand sections, each more or less 820 feet long and 492 feet wide, were lined up around the globe for a total length of more than 25,000 miles. Nearly half the Earth was encircled by Stargraber. It was the greatest human achievement of all time, and the only artificial space object permanently visible to the naked eye from Earth.

Stargraber looked like a string of giant sausages with long, lanky legs grafted on to cling to the Earth. The aligned sections resembled egg-shaped luxury palaces, comparable to London's Gherkin Building, placed on their sides and laid end to end. Similar in size, the elements of this gigantic chain belonged in greater or lesser numbers to the nations behind the project.

The failure of the conquest of space—too costly and complex—had led the states to regroup around a more profitable project. The inexhaustible energy of the sun, enhanced by new technological advances, won unanimous support.

Some of Stargraber's components had very specific functions, while others combined several activities. There were habitation modules, shuttle spaceports and scientific laboratories, but the most remarkable were the station's so-called "one-legged modules". These giant legs were actually elevators that allowed small goods and travellers to access Stargraber quickly, easily and cheaply.

These titanic space elevators consisted of several nanotube cables 31,000 miles long, topped at their ends by counterweights floating in space, weighing several hundred tonnes. All that remained was to move the giant elevators along the cable to reach the station's geostationary orbit, 22,300 miles from Earth.

These one-legged modules had another essential function. They transferred the solar energy harvested by the station back to Earth. To do this, each module of the station was covered with giant photovoltaic panels that moved on three axes facing the sun.

This achievement was made possible by Professor Jeremy Deloy's invention in 2045 of an adaptive force field called "Earth 2", which not only solved Stargraber's gravity problems, but also protected the elevators and the station from micro-meteorites and other space debris.

Meanwhile, Stargraber had grown even larger, encircling nearly the entire 25,000-mile diameter of Earth's surface. The station could accommodate ten million colonists and their families to live, work and even die.

This monumental station was created for two reasons. It was to be a springboard for a new future conquest of space, and to enable Earth to regenerate its fossil fuels by accumulating and using the energy sources present in space—especially solar energy and diffuse deep-sky radiation.

Everyone on the station was hand-picked on a global scale. Scientists, clerics, politicians, engineers, policemen, cooks, chambermaids—every one of them had been rigorously selected, because life on the station was like living in a giant submarine 25,000 miles long. Everyone had to be able to cope with the particular demands of life as a space submariner.

Everyone who lived on Stargraber felt like a pioneer. Everyone liked to think that a new era was opening up before them because of their commitment.

John Desmond had always refused to go up there and live with Isabella, despite the golden bridges the army had given him in his day. To him, life was only worth living on the land where he was born. To hell with money if it meant confining himself to a pressurised sausage.

There was no shortage of money; Isabella came from a wealthy background, and neither of them would have wanted their future children to be born anywhere but on their ranch.

But with Isabella's death, all those plans were gone. He had no reason to remain on Earth. Maybe, he thought, he'd get on with life faster if he were closer to heaven.

So, six months after his tragic accident, John decided to move to Stargraber. It was Isabella's father, General Moore, who found him a position with the station's police force.

He was put in charge of security for the western part of the American section, known as Little California. It consisted of about forty modules covering almost 6.5 miles—enough to fill his days without thinking too much about the past.

8:15 a.m. As John finally emerged from the syrupy fog in which he found himself, he heard the high-pitched chime of his front door. John took his eyes off the vast emptiness of space and made his way to the door.

His flat was divided into two rooms. He crossed his bedroom in a few steps, taking care not to get his feet caught in any of the small piles of dirty laundry that adorned the carpet. A bed, two nightstands and an almost empty wardrobe completed the room's furnishings. Only the satin sheets gave the place a touch of whimsy.

The main room was more welcoming. He had redecorated the small living room in the same style as the one on his Santa Fe ranch.

It was the only room Isabella had no right to be in. He retreated there every day to work or listen to old soul music. Isabella didn't like this old-fashioned music, with its dubious sound quality.

On the walls hung several copies of master paintings, including a Degas that he particularly liked because the artist had the same first name as his great-grandfather, Edgar. Two deep, comfortable couches faced each other in the centre of the room, separated by a coffee table made of caiman skin he had brought back from the Everglades. To the far right, next to an American pool table, was a magnificent mahogany bar, probably carved from the nose of a Riva.

When he reached the centre of the room, John stopped and stared at the wall that separated the living room from his bedroom.

"Tilbert, tell me, who could disturb me at this hour?"

Tilbert was the name of John's personal computer. In fact, it was much more than a computer. Tilbert was a kind of virtual butler. It handled all the administrative aspects of John's life in his apartment: paying bills, managing mail and appointments, and most importantly, keeping the bar stocked.

The appearance of the wall changed in an instant, and a video image of the hallway outside appeared almost immediately.

"It seems to be your second," said a deep, smooth, almost too-human voice.

"He'd better have a good reason for coming to see me at this hour. Send him in, please."

"Yes, sir."

The huge round metal door of the entrance faded into religious silence. Hubert Bronski entered the room tentatively.

"What are you doing here at this hour? Couldn't it wait until I got to the office?"

"Sorry, Chief. It's about Mr Mac Dugan."

"Archi? What's happened to him now?"

John took advantage of the conversation to assess the state of his whisky stock while recycling the previous day's corpses. He paid no attention to young Hubert, thinking that Archi had once again compromised himself on the arm of a young trainee from the science department.

"There's been an accident, sir," the boy continued, stammering. "Mr Mac Dugan is in the infirmary of the medical module."

John stopped and stared at the boy. Hubert Bronski must have been about twenty-one. Tall and chubby, he had failed every exam in his military career except wrestling, where he had excelled thanks to his extraordinary size. His talent with computers had allowed him to join Stargraber Station six months earlier. John had hired him to assist him, with the unspoken goal of finding a workhorse for his administrative duties. What's more, since Bronski's father had worked on the station's technical services for the transfer of solar energy to Earth, John felt obliged to keep him on, at least until the end of his two-year probationary period.

As he met Bronski's gaze, John realised that Bronski was more afraid to tell him the news than to talk about the seriousness of the accident.

"It's serious?" he said, returning to his meticulous inventory count.

"I don't think so, sir."

"You don't think so, or you're sure?"

"I think I'm sure… I mean, yes…"

"Yes, you idiot."

"Yes, uh… Chief."

John rolled his eyes and gave him a disillusioned look, shaking his head.

What an idiot, he thought. *'Chief'—and why not 'my General'?*

Hubert recovered immediately, almost standing to attention.

"I mean, he's fine, but he wants to see you, sir."

"Okay, I'll be right there. In the meantime, go back to the office and take care of business. And no initiative. If you have any problems, call me."

"Yes, sir. Thank you, sir."

Hubert Bronski left the room without looking back, thinking that it had gone rather well.

John followed a few minutes later. On the doorstep, he paused to address Tilbert.

"The whisky's gone, and the brandy's almost empty," said John almost mechanically.

"It will be done, sir. Good day," answered the voice.

The heavy steel door shut behind him.

John took the long corridor that led to the Navigons. The Navigons were internal transporters used to get in and out of the various modules. They could move horizontally or vertically through the different sections, thanks to an ingenious tilting system that did not affect the passengers.

John Desmond settled into Navigon Express number 8. It would take him only a few minutes to cross the six modules that separated him from the Sickbay.

Mac had joined him on the Stargraber after Isabella's death. No doubt he had feared at the time that John might do something foolish if left alone.

His work on the station as an expert in orbital physics, and his degree in nuclear physics, had enabled him to quickly find a position aboard Stargraber. He was responsible for managing the solar energy collected by the station and transferring it to Earth via the one-legged module known as Little California.

Each nation on the station was responsible for one or two one-legged modules. They were also responsible for the daily transfer of solar energy collected by Stargraber back to Earth. Archi Mac

Dugan was in charge of monitoring, maintaining and fine-tuning one of the two American one-legged modules.

The station's position outside Earth's atmosphere gave it far greater collection capacity than photovoltaic panels on the ground. Solar energy was gathered twenty-four hours a day, 365 days a year. When part of Stargraber was in Earth's shadow, its solar panels continued to collect the diffuse energies of the deep sky. This dual function meant that the solar panels were highly efficient.

What's more, the size of the terrestrial infrastructure needed to distribute this energy was greatly reduced. The economic benefits were enormous in the second half of the 21st century. Today, the station is capable of providing all the world's energy needs at such a low cost that it is free.

This radical change in energy supply meant that the Earth was no longer dependent on fossil fuels. The hope of today's scientists was that the Earth would be able to regenerate itself. In the eyes of future generations, Stargraber would be the first human creation capable of providing virtually unlimited free energy.

Arriving at the medical module, John presented himself at the infirmary reception desk.

"Hello, Miss. I'm looking for Archi Mac Dugan, please."

"Room 62," the nurse replied curtly, too busy filling out the week's schedule—or perhaps she had noticed John's disastrous condition.

Arriving at the room, John stood in the doorway, as if to better observe the scene before him.

Archi was standing at the foot of the bed with a drip walker in hand. His arms and legs were tangled in the tubes connecting him to bags of water solution. Two nurses struggled to help him.

"I don't need you," he yelled. "I just want to empty my bladder, and then I don't need any of this. I'm fine, I'm telling you."

"Doctor's orders, Professor," one of the nurses tried.

"He can take his orders where I think they belong," Archi growled, desperately trying to free himself from his bonds.

"It's for your own good," the second nurse continued. "You've gone into shock and need to be rehydrated."

"Need to rehydrate? I'm on my way to the bathroom to empty my bladder. Do you really think I need to be hydrated?"

"The doctor is pretty adamant that you need to be monitored twenty-four hours a day," said the first.

Fluttering around Mac Dugan like panicked white butterflies, the two nurses finally freed him.

John decided to enter.

"My old friend, will you stop pestering these two magnificent creatures?"

"John... Good to see you. Just so you know, those creatures are vampires who want to suck my blood right down to the marrow. Don't ever set foot in here again," Archi said in an annoyed tone.

"Good morning, ladies," said John, surreptitiously glancing at the white outfits of the two nurses. No doubt he thought he finally had the answer to the question men had asked themselves for centuries: *are they naked under their scrubs?*

"Good morning, Monsieur Desmond," they said in unison.

As they left the room, one of them turned back.

"We'll leave him with you in the hope that he'll be more cooperative. We'll be back in an hour for his blood test."

"You see, John? I told you. Vampires are vampires," Archi insisted, still annoyed.

"I'm glad to see you too. But I'd like to know what brought you here," John asked, frowning.

"Sit down, and I'll tell you all about it. This morning, as I was making my usual rounds of the secondary power control transformers, I thought I saw someone lurking near the charging capacitors."

John didn't always understand the technical jargon Archi used. His official title was Director of Power Transfers. In reality, it covered a much broader and more complex area of expertise than it appeared. The DPTs used powerful computers to calculate and regulate the routing of solar energy to Earth. This work was critical, because the accumulators and other capacitors needed to keep the system running smoothly were all connected in series. Given the vast amounts of energy being collected, the slightest error could have a major impact on Earth's energy supply.

The failure of one of the main transformers, whether through miscalculation or poor maintenance, could create anomalies that would affect the entire Stargraber Station. Every day, the DPT had to ensure that each piece of equipment was properly calibrated so that the one-legged module he was responsible for could deliver its daily flow of power to Earth without interruption.

"But when I got there," Archi continued, "I didn't see anyone. I checked that no one had touched the capacitors—everything was fine. The only thing I noticed was a slight power fluctuation, which I quickly corrected. After that, I wanted to leave through the south door—the same way my *rodeur* should have gone out."

"And you didn't see anyone, I suppose?"

"I don't know," Archi said. "I didn't have time to see anything. I barely made it to the boom door—and then I woke up here. The orderly on duty told me it must have been a pneumatic malfunction that knocked the door off its pedestal."

"You know very well that certain parts of this station haven't been maintained in years. The pneumatic security doors have never worked properly. They should have been replaced with a more reliable system long ago."

"No, you're wrong, John. We're talking about a power module here—not some faded enclosure module that nobody cares about.

One-legged modules are the most expensive and technologically advanced. You know as well as I do that their perfect functioning in this part of the station is vital."

John frowned slightly.

"You're probably right. And if it wasn't an accident, it had to be deliberate. But who would want to blow that door down?"

"I have no idea—and that's why I asked you here," Archi replied.

"Who else had access to the module?"

"A lot of maintenance technicians. But I hired them myself. I don't think any of them had anything to do with it. In fact... I don't know. It could be anyone. You know I've never approved of one-legged modules carrying people and power at the same time."

John recoiled slightly, his eyebrows raising against his will. He had just realised that the number of suspects had increased from one to several hundred. Each elevator held fifty passengers. The elevators made twenty trips a day. As far as John was concerned, the count was quick. If the suspect didn't live on the station, he might never find him.

"Listen, Archi—I'm going to get to the bottom of this. If someone did this on purpose, I'll find him."

"On purpose," Archi repeated with a growl. "Do you think I was knocked to the ground by a 440-pound door per set?"

"I didn't say that," John replied. "But we don't even know if it was you or the station that was targeted. Anyway, I'm going to go see what's going on. And while I'm there, think about it. Tell me if you can think of anyone who might have a grudge against you, or who might have an interest in attacking this station's energy transfers."

John patted Archi on the shoulder and left the room. Whoever was responsible for this incident would have to answer to him.

The first thing he decided to do was return to the scene of the disaster and find out just how fertile Archi's imagination could be.

Back on the Navigon Express, John couldn't help but assess the situation. Who on Earth would want to take on Archi? No one could. From his point of view, Archi was loved by everyone—except, of course, the nurses at the medical centre. If there had been any action taken against him, it must have had something to do with the energy transfers.

But it didn't make sense. The Stargraber Project had been approved by the entire world. It had solved energy problems on a global scale. In particular, this free, clean energy had helped resolve world hunger. Extraordinary resources could now be used anywhere in the world to produce, extract, desalinate or process raw materials for the benefit of the most remote populations.

Arriving at the site, John affixed his badge to one of the perimeter security detectors his staff had installed earlier. It displayed a holographic message that scrolled like the yellow stripes used by 20th-century police forces:

Danger. Do not cross.

Once past the detectors, he began to examine what remained of the door. It was 23 feet from its original position. Archi had been very lucky—nothing had prevented him from following the trajectory of the door, which would have crushed him like a pancake.

He retraced his steps and looked at the door frame. The thick rubber bushings that held the door in place had burst, and he had been ejected. As John bent down, a detail caught his eye. A viscous substance had collected near the safety valve, which allowed gas to escape in the event of system overpressure.

At first, he thought it was part of the hydraulic fluid that might have leaked after the explosion. As he rolled the gelatinous liquid between his fingers to better assess it, a doubt crept into his mind. Bringing his fingers to his nostrils, he realised that someone had intentionally blown up this door.

This was no longer an accident.

One of those nano-reactive silicones that could change the properties of steel had been used. These silicones were commonly used to assemble and seal metal parts. The nano-reactive silicone altered the very nature of steel, making it more malleable—almost like rubber—so that certain metal parts could be easily joined together. Once the silicone dissipated, the metal returned to its original properties and the job was done.

Whoever was responsible for the door explosion had used it to weaken the resistance of the gongs and prevent the safety valve from working properly.

John wasn't sure of anything anymore. He had once thought he'd be a driver and die an old man by his wife's side. He thought he'd never live on the station. He thought Archi had no enemies.

He had to admit that his world was changing.

John took a deep breath. Now he had to find out who wanted his friend dead. Why booby-trap the door? Why not attack his friend directly?

It was going to be a long day.

Was this the end of his certainties?

Chapter Two
A Breathtaking View

In the heart of the New Mexico Plateau, the underground galleries of Afterone, named for their sudden creation during the Big One of 2112, were a treasure trove for opportunists of all kinds.

They had been formed by molten magma escaping from the bowels of the Earth through conduits created by the earthquake. These conduits had been emptied of their magma before being cooled by violent gas explosions, creating large galleries, some several feet in diameter.

On the surface, an entire microcosm of scientists, geologists, treasure hunters, apprentice adventurers and speleologists had taken up residence across much of the plateau, creating a kind of post-apocalyptic mining town, far removed from the surrounding modernity.

Victoria Palmers had a concession south of New Eldorado City, the best place to find "green" gold and selenium. This precious metal had become highly sought after since it was used in Stargraber's solar panels.

She had inherited the concession from her father, who had died a few years earlier, and managed her workers in an almost family atmosphere.

The concession was located at the top of a hill, giving her an unobstructed view of the entire city of New Eldorado. The city stretched for over seven miles from north to south and consisted mostly of haphazard structures built by the newcomers. On the horizon, from Victoria's concession, one could see one of the two American one-legged modules.

Each district of this unlikely city had a precise function. From south to north: the miners' district came first, followed by the ore processing area. Next was the commercial district—the most important zone—and finally, the shipping zone, which also included a tourist area for adventurers seeking a thrill.

"I wish I had the idiot who turned off the ventilation," shouted Sergio, Victoria's foreman, as he came up from the mine.

The entrance to the mine was at the top of the hill. It was formed by a natural chimney that had been used to vent gases and gave direct access to a large number of galleries.

"What's going on, my friend?" said Victoria.

"It's hot as hell, Mademoiselle, and suddenly there's no light either. Someone must have turned off the power somewhere. We can't go on like this—this is the third time this month."

In fact, just a few minutes after the last of the concession's workers had climbed out of the chimney of the extraction shaft, there had been a great blast of heat accompanied by a slight tremor. The heat wave was so intense that it blurred the horizon, like a mirage in the heart of the desert, making the leg of the one-legged module dance in the distance.

"But the ventilation is working. I checked it ten minutes ago," said Victoria. "Then we'll call it a day. Whatever happens, I've got to get to the Jones District before closing to negotiate this month's sale."

"With all these setbacks, this probably won't be our best run," Sergio replied. "But it's just a temporary issue. Tomorrow will be better."

"Tomorrow you'll be in charge of the concession, because I have to go to Stargraber to evaluate a drilling machine for Mars."

"You, Miss? On Stargraber for a drilling operation on Mars? I'm surprised at you! Are you sure you understood them correctly?"

"Yes, I understand. But you're right—this is the first time I'll have set foot on the station. I don't want to spend my whole life locked up in those tin cans. And knowing that all our energy depends on them scares me. As for interplanetary travel, I thought that was a thing of the past. But they gave me a golden bridge. They said that my work made me one of the few people qualified to, and I quote, 'anticipate future failures of the Mars drilling system.'"

"And you believed them?" interrupted Sergio.

"All I know," she continued, "is that if I accept, they'll extend my concession licence for three years, free of charge, so... And please don't doubt my abilities. Didn't I design the head of our current drill?"

"Yes, Miss—but with the help of your father, may he rest in peace. Besides, they want to drill on Mars, not in loose tunnels on Earth."

"Thank you for your concern, but I'll be fine. I'll take this opportunity to go and see the person in charge of energy to find out if their activities could be disrupting the environment of our tunnels and causing these heat waves."

"All right, Miss. I'll see you in forty-eight hours. I'll finish packing up the extraction equipment and go home," Sergio concluded.

The sun was beginning to set as Victoria made her way to the Jones District. The place was named after the Dow Jones of Wall Street in the last century. It was here that all the transactions—the buying and selling of ore—took place.

By this time, most of the merchants were already closed. Since New Eldorado City was not meant to be permanent, it had been built with bricks and mortar. Most of the buildings were made of various materials and containers scattered here and there.

The main building, the only one that appeared to be open, seemed disproportionately large compared to the rest of the surrounding structures. It was clearly made up of several units—a sort of "porta-cabin" stacked one atop the other over the years. It belonged to the oldest resident, Buba Kellnik, a chubby man with a keen business sense.

Buba was the first to see the value of this new gallery location. In his early twenties, with the help of his father, he was the first to obtain a concession from the government to exploit the contents uncovered by the creation of the Afterone galleries.

Having no scientific or geological knowledge, he had negotiated a contract that all future transactions would go through him. The sole purpose of his concession was to centralise transactions and take a large commission in the process.

Victoria didn't particularly like the man, but she was forced to put on a brave face for him in order to maintain her hard-earned perks. Buba had seen her grow up here when she used to accompany her father, and he had grown quite fond of her—offering her privileges that only a handful of residents could hope for.

It wasn't difficult for Victoria to make the most of her advantages. Her father had taught her well, and nature hadn't forgotten her either. She was nearly five feet tall, dark-haired with green eyes, and her long legs were matched only by her slender waist. However, she only played on those assets on rare occasions. A bit of a tomboy around the edges, she preferred to use her brains to get things done — a well-made mind in a more than perfect body.

It wasn't with Buba, however, that she would use her charms. He was far too old, fat and devious for her. Victoria liked directness and always got right to the point. Besides, she had always had her doubts about her father's accident.

Buba had been present when the gallery collapsed, killing the man who had taught her everything and whom she had loved so much — and Buba had been too vague about the circumstances of the tragedy. Too young at the time, she hadn't been able to find out more. Afterwards, Buba had always been open with her, almost protective. That was enough to calm her doubts.

Known as the White Wolf, Victoria used to enter Buba's house unannounced.

"Anyone home?" she called into what looked like an entrance hall.

The place was cosy, consisting of a small main building to which various extensions had been added over the years — a sort of giant adult Lego.

"Buba, are you there? We need to talk..." No reply.

Moving through the hall, Victoria thought she heard a noise coming from one of the adjoining rooms. Through the translucent partitions, she recognised Buba's squat form. As she approached, the sounds became clearer. Sounds became words, and words became sentences.

Conspiracy... Implosion... destruction... death... Little California... If it happened, it could be... The greatest genocide mankind has ever known... We have to do it... We all agree, in three days we act... The ISS Stargraber will be our target...

Horrified, Victoria recognised Buba's voice among the two others she couldn't identify. She immediately decided to turn back, not yet fully aware of what she had just heard. But she knew she shouldn't stay there. All of her receptors had turned red.

As she turned back as discreetly as possible, the words clashed in her head: death, genocide, destroy Stargraber. Had she heard right?

Suddenly, as she turned, Victoria found herself face to face with Buba's cat, Sécotine. Surprised, she let out a muffled cry from the back of her throat.

The three companions fell silent. Victoria suspected she had been discovered.

Shit, she thought.

"It's only the cat," Buba said to his two companions. "Go check it out and bring it back to me."

The two men left the back office and headed for the lobby.

When she heard the office door open, Victoria's adrenaline surged.

If they find me here, I'm finished, she told herself. **Buba's friendship won't save me this time. If they want to attack the ISS and destroy it, they'll probably have no reason to spare me.**

She instinctively decided to flee as quickly and as far as possible — and think about it later. In her haste, she knocked over a water jug on the reception desk at the entrance. This time, Buba's companions were certain it wasn't the cat and hurried to the entrance.

Before stepping out, Victoria turned up the collar of her jacket and tucked her long hair under her cap to disguise her femininity. Maybe she'd stand a chance in the crowd?

When she reached the street, she began to run in the direction of her claim. Suddenly, she slowed down, regained her composure for a moment, and decided to walk.

Now, keep walking, she told herself. **Slowly, calmly, don't turn back.**

Fear was gripping her every second. The more she tried to be discreet, the more she felt as though a hand might come over her shoulder and stop her. The pressure was too great. Without realising it, she finally turned around to see if she was being followed.

Meanwhile, Buba had joined his men at the door and was scanning the surrounding streets for the intruder.

Victoria stealthily met Buba's gaze and acted as if nothing had happened. She continued on her way, taking the first street to the right, then one to the left, retracing her steps two streets back, and finally stopping in a little-used alley.

Shit, he saw me... I shouldn't have turned around. I'm sure he recognised me. He'll be looking for me. I've got to go back and tell Sergio at the concession.

Buba, who had seen that bewitching look so many times, knew that only Victoria could have come at this late hour to negotiate the sale of her ore. What had she heard? He couldn't take any chances. The stakes were too high. He had to find her.

All she could do, he thought, was return to her claim and ask her foreman for help. There was no point in chasing her; he'd find her there.

Victoria would have liked to warn Sergio of her arrival so he could prepare her escape. Unfortunately, modern means of communication such as Gcom tended to interact unpredictably with the explosives used in the basements. As a result, all long-range electronic transmitters were banned from New Eldorado and had to be deactivated upon arrival in the transit zone.

Knowing the city like no one else, Victoria knew she'd get there on foot before Buba, who, given his overweight frame, could only get around by Transplace. The Transplace was very practical — a kind of small automated vehicle that travelled from neighbourhood to neighbourhood, always on the move and without a driver, allowing passengers to get in and out wherever they pleased. Its only disadvantage was its relative slowness.

With this slight advantage, Victoria was the first to arrive at the concession. Her offices were located at the bottom of the hill, with a direct view of the mining shaft. A little out of breath, she pushed the door open with all her might.

"Sergio, stop at once. We're leaving," she said.

"I'm sorry, Miss," Sergio replied with a look of astonishment. "I still have to put away the—"

"No time," Victoria interrupted. "Get your things and go to your family in New York. We're in big trouble."

Sergio was used to Victoria surprising him, but this time, she seemed more nervous than usual. Still, he trusted her enough to do what she asked.

"And your appointment on the ISS? You're not going? It seemed very important to you."

"It still is—more than ever, my friend. In fact, I think it's my only chance of not being discovered by young explorers at the bottom of one of my galleries in a hundred years or so."

"Aren't you exaggerating a bit, Mademoiselle Victoria?"

"No, Sergio, the situation is as serious as I make it out to be. I don't want to involve you. All you need to know is that I overheard a conversation when I went to see Buba, and I think he saw me spying on him and is looking for me."

"It's not that bad. Just talk to him, and he'll understand you weren't spying on him willingly. Mr Kellnik adores you—he's your friend. I'm sure he'll let it go."

"No, Sergio. What I've heard no longer puts him in the 'friend' category. But I can tell you it has something to do with Stargraber. I've got to get over there and get some help. Unfortunately, I'm sure Buba will be here any minute to intercept me. Before you go, I need your help. I need a diversion."

"Tell me what to do," Sergio said.

"You're going to put my overalls and cap on the dummy we used to test the fire resistance of our new suits and climb up to the well at the top of the concession. From there, you'll have a great view and be able to see Buba coming. Place the dummy on the ladder leading down to the shaft, with its head bent over the opening.

"Then wait for Kellnik to arrive. When he sees the doll at the bottom of the hill, he'll think he's seen me chatting with one of my employees as he climbs back up."

"That won't save you much time, Mademoiselle."

"That's right—except that before you slip away, you'll have to drop this piece of dynamite into the shaft opening. If my calculations are correct, the opening should collapse under the force of the explosion, engulfing the dummy in a pile of rubble. Buba won't know what hit him. He'll think that you were carrying explosives on your way up and that you got caught in one of those heat waves that have been building up for some time."

Victoria smiled slightly, obviously proud of her little diversion. Sergio, on the other hand, was less convinced. Since the galleries were relatively unstable, this little trick might prove to be more uncontrollable than expected.

Victoria took cover behind a rock, far enough away to watch the action unfold without being spotted.

Buba arrived a few minutes later, accompanied by his two companions. It didn't take more than a second for Kellnik to spot the dummy near the well. About 350 feet from where they had arrived, the three of them began to climb towards the decoy Sergio had placed. From the bottom of the small hill, it really looked like Victoria was standing there, waiting for someone to come out of the well.

Halfway up the hill, Buba stopped for a moment to catch his breath. Exercise wasn't his forte—he preferred drunken meals where he could brag about his latest acquisitions. Victoria told herself that everything was going like clockwork and that the explosion would happen at any moment.

Without resuming his ascent, Buba yelled at the mannequin, no doubt hoping to get Victoria's attention so he wouldn't have to finish climbing the hill.

Three, two, one... Victoria counted in her head.

Nothing happened.

With no response, Buba decided to carry on as best he could. Exasperated by the effort, he sent his two accomplices forward to bring back his prey as quickly as possible.

"Still nothing," Victoria worried.

At least, she thought, Sergio must have had enough time to escape. On the other hand, if it didn't go off right away, there could be real casualties, assuming—

A huge jolt snapped Victoria out of her thoughts. The dynamite in the gallery had just exploded. As Victoria had predicted, the entrance to the gallery had swallowed the mannequin before Buba's men arrived.

The icing on the cake was that Buba had lost his balance during the tremor and literally rolled to the bottom of the concession. Victoria couldn't help but laugh inwardly as she watched him struggle to his feet—and slip again. Looking at the collapsed top of the concession, Buba seemed dejected. His companions joined him, and a heated discussion ensued between the three men before they finally left the site.

Bad timing for terrorists, she thought. **Now that they think I'm dead, I can leave without them looking for me. I have some time to find help and stop them from attacking the station.**

How do I get to the station? she wondered.

Victoria knew she couldn't use the elevators in Little California's one-legged module. No doubt Buba would try to enter the station from there.

The only option was to go to the New Eldorado Spaceport. The city's transit and shipping district served as a commercial link to the station, as well as a tourist rallying point. In the midst of the tourists, Victoria would undoubtedly go unnoticed and could probably pass herself off as an escort for some space tourist group.

She was finally going to do what she'd always dreamed of—pose as a secret agent. Inside, Victoria couldn't wait.

I need to find a man—preferably one with a face like this—and propose to him...

Suddenly, her wrist vibrated. It was her Gcom, which had been reactivated behind the transit zone.

It was the newest means of communication. An implant behind the ear made it possible to speak to or hear a correspondent. The Gcom chip could be integrated into a watch, a pair of glasses, or even a ring for the ladies. Everything was controlled by gestures and voice.

Convenient and efficient, communication had become as natural as breathing. However, most people still wore a personalised wristband that contained the Gcom chip. Despite all technological advances, people continued to put their hands to their ears—if only to signal they were on a call and avoid looking like madmen talking to themselves.

"Hello, this is Victoria Palmers."

"Hi, I'm John Desmond, Head of Security for Little California. I understand you have an appointment with Gerald Bedford at the station tomorrow?"

"Hello, uh..." Victoria was surprised. No one was supposed to call her back to confirm the appointment. "Yes, that's right. I'm listening."

"Mr Bedford asked me to make sure you have everything you need when you arrive. Do you want me to send a shuttle for you, or are you coming alone?"

Disappointed and delighted at the same time, Victoria told herself that even James Bond was entitled to public transport.

"I haven't had much time to myself lately, and I thought I'd take the express elevators to the one-legged module tomorrow, but I don't have a ticket yet."

"The shuttle will be more comfortable," John added. "Besides, the wait can be hell during rush hour. What time do you want me to pick you up?"

"Can I ask you a favour?"

"Please do."

Victoria was a little embarrassed to be abusing her new VIP status so soon, but she couldn't reasonably spend the night on the tarmac.

"I was wondering," she continued, "if I could spend the night at the station. I've never been there, and I want to make the most of this short stay."

"Don't worry, Madame—"

"Mademoiselle," Victoria interrupted.

"Not to worry, Mademoiselle," John replied. "I can have a shuttle there within the hour. I'll book you a room at the Starview. You won't be able to count the stars from here," he added, hoping for a reaction.

"Thank you. I'll see you at the New Eldorado Spaceport in an hour," she concluded.

Deep in thought and relieved to have found a way out, Victoria didn't notice Desmond's tentative attempt to lighten the mood.

"Very well, Miss. In one hour. Goodbye."

A certain annoyance began to creep over John. He hated being the puppy dog for the station's VIPs. First of all, he'd never heard of this Victoria Palmers—and he was well acquainted with the closed world of VIPs likely to board Stargraber. Besides, she didn't seem like much fun, he thought. A star-studded hotel on a space station was ridiculous. Still, she could have reacted!

"Well... there are worse things," he reassured himself. Besides, it shouldn't take too long to park her in the hotel for the night.

It was already late. The shuttle was supposed to arrive before 22:30. By the time he had booked the room and made his way to the Naviport, John was running out of time.

The shuttle left at about 10 p.m. Victoria was seated by a window in a wide, full-grain leather seat with an ergonomic headrest. A hostess immediately offered her a glass of champagne and some petits fours in a soufflé that hadn't even had time to settle.

Top of the line, she said to herself. **They really know how to make you feel good.**

The launch was very smooth. With the mastery of ion engines, it was now possible to take off in the conventional way and reach space as easily as flying from New York to Miami. The "Earth 2" artificial gravity system was activated when the shuttle reached the edge of space, so the passengers did not experience weightlessness.

Once in sight of the station, Victoria was stunned by the spectacle before her. Alone in the shuttle, she wished someone had accompanied her to describe what she was seeing through the porthole. She had only ever seen the station from the ground. She had seen it through her telescope, like everyone else—but now the full significance of this unprecedented human achievement struck her.

As if to better acquaint her with the station, the shuttle whirled around the modules at a seemingly reasonable speed. Victoria had time to take in every detail of the structure.

The modules were beautiful—at least, more so than she had imagined. They were a tangle of polished steel and aluminium, embedded with large glass panels. They sparkled on all sides in the reflection of the sun. It was as if the Earth contained a river of diamonds.

When the shuttle passed to the land side of the station, hidden from the sun, the view was different but just as fascinating. This time, you could literally see through the station. Every detail of station life was revealed. The living quarters were warm and inviting—something for everyone's taste. Normal life seemed to flow quietly. Through a window, you could see people going about their business. A veritable anthill bustled before your eyes.

The modules lined up as far as the eye could see in a perfect curve, looking ridiculously small on the horizon—stark in contrast to the gigantism of the whole. Still, Victoria felt uneasy that Earth's energy supply depended on a structure that looked so fragile compared to the immensity of the void that surrounded it.

This thought resonated within her, and Victoria began to reflect on the events she had just experienced.

Why would Buba Kellnik want to attack Stargraber Station? Sure, he was a hustler and a profiteer, but he wasn't an assassin—

and he certainly didn't seem capable of organising a large-scale attack. Could she be so wrong about him? She had to be on her guard. She lacked information, and everything felt confused.

And then there were the heat waves over the past few weeks. None of them seemed natural to her. She needed to talk to the right people to understand where she stood.

John arrived at the Naviport with the precision of a Swiss watch. As he arrived, Victoria's transport had just landed.

The arrival hangar was impressive, even for the natives. The gaping hole in the station's structure gave the constant impression that the vacuum of space could suck you in at any moment. A double force field allowed vehicles to enter and exit without the need for a decompression airlock. In addition to being a spectacular sight, the system was fast and efficient. The shuttles seemed to move in and out of the hangar like helicopters leaving their helipads.

The VIP shuttles were parked in a special part of the Naviport. The location ensured that visitors did not feel out of place from the moment they arrived. The cargo area—the main activity of the Naviport—was separated from the VIP arrival area by opaque, variable-geometry walls. This optical effect made the area where the Navips (as the handlers called them) were stationed seem equally imposing and avoided the claustrophobic feeling one might expect while working there.

As Victoria stepped out of the machine, John mechanically straightened up, as if to better introduce himself.

"John Desmond. Good evening, Miss. I'm pleased to welcome you to Stargraber." His eyes instinctively scanned the silhouette of his interlocutor. Victoria's natural charm had not escaped him.

"Good evening, thank you. My name is Victoria Palmers."

Victoria felt herself blushing. *He called me... he has my file. Of course he knows my name.*

"I'll show you to your cabin," John said.

"Thanks, I'd love to. I'm a bit tired; I've had a busy day."

Aboard the Navigon that took them to the VIP quarters, John set about breaking the ice.

"How did your climb go?"

"Yes, thank you, it was very educational. I was a little embarrassed to be a voyeur at times."

"I don't blame you. There aren't many shuttles that make the grand tour, as we call it. Curtains on the windows aren't mandatory here. But I assure you, there are always curtains in the VIP areas."

Victoria smiled slightly.

"May I ask what your speciality is? There's nothing in your file except your name."

"I hope they didn't write down my age?" Victoria worried.

"No, I assure you," John replied with an amused look.

"I'm a jack of all trades, but I specialise in onshore drilling. My father left me a selenium concession near New Eldorado."

"Very impressive. I hear it's a tough job. At the end of the day, you contribute to the smooth running of this station—and Earth. Without you, there would be no solar panels."

"And why are you here, if you don't mind me asking? Do you need to check the quality of our solar panels?"

"Not at all, but I'd like to meet the person in charge of the energy transfer to Earth. I'm very interested."

For the moment, Victoria was hiding the real reason she wanted to meet the DPT. She didn't know whom she could trust. Maybe she could at least get some answers about the heat waves that had hit her mines.

"I'll take care of that, Mademoiselle."

"In fact, I'm here to contribute my experience in drilling. Apparently, they want to resume exploration of the Martian subsurface."

John was astonished.

"These programmes were abandoned nearly fifty years ago when Stargraber enabled Earth to become energy self-sufficient. At the time, it was felt that our technology couldn't make such long journeys profitable. Stargraber became a government priority. They preferred to ensure the sustainability of inexhaustible energy and make it available to all, rather than set out to conquer our solar system.

"Stargraber became a project of all nations, and its production was such that energy would be free by 2140. The nations decided to redirect their space programmes to basic research—to find more efficient means of propulsion and shorten travel times. That was the *sine qua non* for the possibility of establishing a contingent on Mars.

"If the engineers haven't come up with a new type of stellar engine, I didn't think it was possible for us to return to Mars. It's been years since I've heard anything even remotely resembling a Mars project."

"I agree with you. But on the one hand, this story has piqued my curiosity, and on the other hand, they're going to pay me handsomely—so here I am."

Just then, a soft, almost too-human voice sounded: "Next stop, VIP area B9 through B12."

"This is it," said John.

The VIP quarters were worthy of the finest five-star hotels in the world. Mumbai—the luxury capital of the world—was clearly the benchmark.

The rarest woodwork was juxtaposed with the finest fabrics. The 2.4-metre-wide bed in the bedroom looked almost small in the vast room it occupied.

As for the living room, it could have held a basketball court—if it hadn't been filled with a huge bookcase, a snooker table, and a grand piano, all three originals probably dating from the 20th century.

Only one word came out of Victoria's mouth: "Waouh."

"You'll get used to it," John commented. Then he added, "Personalised room service twenty-four hours a day, Jacuzzi, direct access to strategic points of the resort, and to top it all off—curtains on all the windows. I hope you enjoy your stay with us."

Victoria didn't need to smile; her face had been expressive ever since she entered the penthouse.

"I'll send you your appointment times and directions on your Visicom."

The Visicom was a software extension of the Gcom that allowed all kinds of documents to be sent or received, and displayed on the communicating parts of objects or walls in the immediate environment. Most furniture or walls in a home had modular surfaces that could be converted into multitasking communication panels.

"Thank you for your concern. See you tomorrow," Victoria concluded.

She walked over to one of the huge picture windows, opened the curtains, and found that, indeed, it was a breathtaking view.

Chapter Three
Thanks Dad

The next morning, John was sitting at his desk, recovering from a night of drinking that had gone a little too far, with a cup of coffee so dry that his teaspoon almost stood up on its own in the cup.

"Still in the juice?" Archi said as he stepped through the door.

"Hello to you too, Archi. What's new?"

"Well, I've got an appointment with a guy named Palmers this morning. The old man said I should show him our facilities and explain how we transfer energy and blah-blah-blah... Who does Bedford think he is? I'm not a tour guide! Besides, right now, after the attempt on my life, I'm dealing with heightened security and checking all the equipment. I don't have a second to spare."

"First of all, I've already told you not to call him 'the old man'. Bedford is our boss and he's no older than you are. He runs this part of the station, and I think he deserves a little respect. Second—and this should please you—Palmers is not a man. She's a beautiful brunette with green eyes."

"Bedford can go to hell. He didn't lift a finger after my assassination attempt. Let me remind you that I got hit in the face with a door weighing several hundred pounds. He could have at least started a serious investigation instead of just increasing security."

"But he did! He asked me to get to the bottom of it, and so far I've come up with nothing. You know very well that I spare no effort—especially when it comes to a friend. Apart from the fact that the door was sabotaged, which I quickly discovered, I don't have anything else. Your attacker left no clues. I know this case makes you nervous, but please let me do my job and stop attacking me so early in the morning."

"All right then. I'll go and get this Palmers, but on your side, give me some room. All this heightened security—guards everywhere—it's stressful. I can't even pee by myself anymore."

"I don't understand you. Two minutes ago, you were complaining that Bedford wasn't doing enough, and now you're telling me you're too protected." John started to get annoyed; it wasn't in Archi's nature to be so fickle.

"I'm just saying the problem isn't with me," Archi continued. "I don't mind tightening security, but if you're going to follow me around all day like I'm the saboteur, I say stop it!"

"All right, I'll see what I can do. But I reserve the right to take care of your security myself."

"All right. I'll leave you to it. I'm going to be late for your client's sightseeing tour."

As soon as he'd finished his sentence, Archi left, scowling.

"A thank you would have been nice," John said to the already closed door.

A moment later, a distant "Thank you!" was heard. John smiled slightly as he dove back into his files.

Victoria, in her presidential suite, had taken the time she usually denied herself. She had woken up around 9:30, enjoyed a breakfast in bed worthy of the finest palaces, and an indecently long hot shower.

She arrived a good fifteen minutes late to meet Gerald Bedford, manager of the American West side of Stargraber Station.

Invited in by his secretary, Victoria entered Bedford's office without any preconceptions. It was her first appointment at the station, and John's welcome had been quite good. The place was simple but tasteful. You could tell the man liked being there and didn't count his hours.

The Little California manager's office received no special treatment. The décor was minimalist. The only eye-catcher was a goldfish on the desk—probably Stargraber's only pet. The relative lack of space on the station left little room for imagination. However, everyone had done their best to give their workstations a more human touch.

"Please come in, Miss Palmers."

"Thank you, Mr Bedford. I'm sorry I'm late, but your VIP quarters are perfect for relaxing."

"On the contrary—they make me happy. I see my investment has not been in vain. How do you like Little California?"

"To tell you the truth, I was surprised. I thought I'd find myself in a more austere place, worthy of the best science fiction Z-series, but the whole thing has a certain charm."

"We couldn't live here otherwise," Bedford agreed.

"How can I help you?" Victoria asked again.

"I've asked you here for a very specific reason..."

"I was led to believe that you wanted to know if your drills would be able to dig on Mars," Victoria interrupted.

"Not quite, Mademoiselle. First of all, I need your discretion."

Victoria was a bit surprised. She began to study her interlocutor, as if trying to get a better read on him.

Gerald Bedford was a man in his sixties, with greying temples, a straight forehead and a sturdy build. Although he had no formal education, his leadership skills had allowed him to rise through the ranks of the army. After retiring from military service, he chose the ISS as his new challenge. For him, running such a facility was a military operation.

"I need you," Bedford continued, "for your knowledge of terrestrial geology."

This time, Victoria's face flushed with surprise.

"My geological knowledge?"

"Yes, Miss. As you may have noticed while working in your mines, we're having some... how shall I put it... energy surges at the moment."

"You call the heatwaves that nearly fried three of my men like merguez sausages 'surges'? I'd call that unprofessional."

"Indeed, I understand your anger. I hope your men are okay," Bedford said, seemingly apologetic. "At this point, we don't know what caused the malfunction. Our DPT, Mr Mac Dugan, has not yet located the source of the problem."

Victoria interrupted him again.

"I have an appointment with him today, so I'll see if I can get some useful information out of him."

"Does he know the reason for your visit?" Bedford asked.

"No, I haven't told him. It was your head of security, Mr Desmond, who made the appointment for me."

"Don't tell him. I don't want anyone to know the real reason for your visit. If Mr Mac Dugan finds out why I've asked you here, he'll be very sensitive. He'll think I don't trust him, that I'm trying to protect my own interests—and he'll cause me more problems than he'll solve.

"On the other hand, if word gets out that Stargraber Station— which hasn't had any major problems since it became operational—

is sending out uncontrolled power spikes, I'll let you judge the consequences."

"I know what you mean."

Victoria felt overwhelmed by a vague fear. She had no reason to be afraid, but her instincts, combined with her knowledge of the terrain, made her think the situation was not as harmless as it appeared.

"I wonder what I'll tell Professor Mac Dugan?" she continued.

"Tell him you'd like to meet the person in charge of the solar panels you helped build. That will flatter his ego without drawing attention to yourself. But more than that, I need you to help him determine and understand why these energy spikes are occurring," Bedford replied.

"I don't mind, but I'm stepping out of my area of expertise. Basically, I was the one who was looking for answers."

"If we work together, I think we can get better leads," Bedford insisted. "It'll only take you a morning. Then we'll let you get back to work. You're a civilian, and I want to keep your involvement to a minimum.

"Now—what can you tell me about the effect of these heatwaves on the resistance of the Earth's crust?"

"You may not like my answer."

"Anything you say," Bedford replied impatiently.

"As things stand, nothing catastrophic should happen—except a few second-degree burns to miners in New Eldorado City. These heatwaves are local, and are only being generated by a single one-legged module: yours. But I suppose you already knew that?"

"My men in the field saw it," Bedford confirmed.

"On the other hand," Victoria continued, "if the phenomenon were to multiply over several modules, the Earth's crust could get more than a few shocks."

"What do you mean?" said Bedford, who seemed to fear her answer.

"There are several factors to consider: the intensity, the frequency, and the number of one-legged modules affected by these malfunctions. If all three factors increase simultaneously, the Earth's crust will weaken and temperatures will rise significantly.

"The consequences would be manifold—earthquakes, tsunamis, droughts, floods... the whole panoply of plagues we fear. But I can't say to what extent this would happen."

"My fears were well-founded. We were close to disaster. But you've reassured me that the malfunction only affected Little California. My counterparts in the other modules have confirmed that everything is normal.

"The plagues you're talking about—if they were to occur— would only be comparable to what Earth experiences naturally every year. At most, we could speak of a black year with significant damage, but not apocalyptic, as you imply. Still, I prefer to know the worst so I can anticipate it."

"I haven't told you the worst yet," Victoria continued. "There's a fourth factor to consider: coordination."

"Coordination?" said Bedford, a little taken aback.

"If the factors I've mentioned were to increase simultaneously and in a coordinated fashion, the power of the energy spikes would multiply exponentially. They would add up, and the surface temperature would become unbearable to the human body. This could literally toast the Earth's crust—like bread in a toaster."

"You mean if they weren't accidental?"

"Absolutely, sir."

Victoria paused to watch Bedford's reaction. But he didn't show it.

Why should Bedford react at all? she thought.

"I know enough. Thank you, Miss. I hope we find the source of the problem soon—but it's comforting to know that the consequences have been minimal so far."

"That's not all, sir," Victoria said, with a serious look on her face.

"Please, Mademoiselle. I'm all ears," said Bedford, who would have been quite satisfied with the answer she had just given him.

"I mentioned this fourth factor for a reason."

"Go on—you intrigue me."

"Well, I was supposed to be on board the station for only an hour. I arrived last night because I had to.

"Late yesterday afternoon, I overheard a conversation that made my blood run cold. I only heard bits and pieces of it, but it mentioned a possible attack that would cause many casualties—and it involved Stargraber, and more specifically, Little California.

"At first, I thought the station was their only target. But our conversation about these heatwaves made me think that attacking the station might be just the first step."

"Do you know the people involved?"

"Yes, and they chased me all the way to the mine, where I managed to escape with the help of my foreman."

"And do these people you know seem capable of such an action? I mean, are they capable of organising a simultaneous attack on all the one-legged modules and coordinating their malfunction to create a major planetary catastrophe?"

"When you put it like that, I don't think so," Victoria replied sheepishly. "But I clearly heard that the station would be their target."

"I think you may have misinterpreted what you heard. Still, I never take any chances when it comes to the station. I'll need a description of these men. Then I'll take the necessary steps to increase security at the main access points.

"I'll stop them—if they make the mistake of showing themselves."

"In light of this new information, I repeat my request for your discretion. In my opinion, the station's future could be threatened more by the panic caused by rumours than by possible sabotage attempts."

"I understand, sir."

"You said you knew these people. Do you have any names?"

"Buba Kellnik. I believe he is their leader, but I don't know the names of his accomplices."

"This will allow us to move forward. I'll take it up with my Head of Security. He'll investigate this Kellnik. In the meantime, go to your appointment with Mr Mac Dugan before you return to Earth. Don't worry—the station is secure."

"Thank you, sir. And if you don't need me anymore, I'll take my leave. I'm late for my appointment with Mr Mac Dugan."

"Thank you. Good day, Miss Palmers."

As Victoria opened the door to leave the office, she found herself face to face with Archi Mac Dugan. Surprised and a little nervous, she let out a small cry.

"Professor Mac Dugan, you're just in time," Bedford said. "Miss Palmers was on her way to your office."

Victoria stepped aside to let Archi in.

"Yes, I know all about it, Gerald," Archi said as he entered. "That's why I'm here."

"Hello, Professor," Victoria said, pleased.

"Good morning, Mademoiselle. As I didn't see you arrive, I decided to come here to save you an unnecessary journey.

"I'm afraid I can't see you now. John thought he was doing the right thing by arranging for you to meet me—he probably thought it would distract me—but with recent events, I don't have a minute to myself."

"I'm sorry, Professor. I was looking forward to discussing the effects of selenium in solar panels with you."

"I'm sorry, Miss Palmers," Archi continued. "I'd like to do it another time."

"Gerald," he said, turning to Bedford as if to close the subject, "we need to discuss some important details."

Bedford, not wanting to make Archi wonder any more than necessary, discreetly signalled to Victoria that their appointment had just been cancelled.

"Thank you for your availability, Mademoiselle Palmers," Bedford added. "I am sorry for the inconvenience. I suggest you go to Mr Desmond's office—he'll make the necessary arrangements for your return to Earth. I'll inform him of your arrival."

In the Navigon that took her back to Desmond's office, Victoria, disappointed at not getting the answers she wanted, had the uncomfortable feeling of being followed. Even after being reassured by Bedford about the seriousness of the energy spikes and the possibility of an attack, she still couldn't shake the thought that Buba might already be on the station to carry out his plan.

After stopping by Desmond's office and explaining that her appointment had been cancelled, Victoria and John both headed back to the VIP quarters to collect their suitcases and toothbrushes. On the way, Victoria could not shake the feeling of being watched.

"I have a strange feeling," she said.

"You're not feeling well?" John asked.

"No. It's nothing. Let's keep going."

Victoria knew she shouldn't draw attention to herself.

They were not far from the Naviport. One more Navigon to go, and Victoria would be on the shuttle that would take her back to Earth.

A little patience, she told herself. *After all, I'm well accompanied.*

Arriving at the Navigon stop, an unpleasant surprise awaited them. A large, hastily written sign announced that the Navigon was undergoing maintenance.

"Maintenance!" exclaimed John. "This is the first time they've done this during the day, and nobody told me. Believe me, they'll hear from me!" he ranted. "I'm sorry, Mademoiselle, but we're going to have to make a detour—and it's going to take a little longer.

There's another station on Track B, about fifty feet from here. If we go through the passageways, we won't lose too much time."

"I'll be right behind you."

"You'll find this interesting—you're going to see behind the scenes, Mademoiselle."

"If we're going into the bowels of this station, I think you can call me Victoria. 'Le Mademoiselle' is annoying in the long run."

As soon as she finished her sentence, John opened a door hidden behind a technical panel. After passing through a narrow corridor, John and Victoria found themselves in a much larger room, criss-crossed by a multitude of networks, pipes and cables used to power the station. Here and there, pipes were leaking, and a few poorly sheathed cables gave off the occasional spark. Every fifty to seventy feet were two staircases leading to the upper and lower decks. In the middle of this vast space was a large tube, about thirty-five feet in diameter, through which the Navigons passed.

"Impressive, but messy," Victoria said. "I finally feel like I'm on a real space station," she added, trying to lighten the mood.

Victoria still had that uncomfortable, nagging feeling—and this place wasn't helping.

"This is one of the oldest parts of the station," John continued. "In the 21st century, we built it solid. It was made to last—and as you can see, much of the equipment from that time is still in use.

Nowadays we'd use self-repairing nanomaterials, but I find this place has a certain old-fashioned charm."

"It's not very comforting... and that deafening noise..." Victoria shouted to cover the sound.

A Navigon had just passed through the adjacent tube.

"I'm afraid you're right. I'm as concerned as you are, Miss—er, Victoria. As far as we know, this Navigon should be stopped for maintenance. My instincts aren't right."

"Ah... you too?" Victoria replied. "Thank you very much. I feel less alone now."

No sooner had she finished her sentence than two explosions echoed through the room, followed by a multitude of others.

"And what was that?" said Victoria, clutching John's arm.

"Gunshots. Get down," John ordered, pulling her arm back. "Stay behind this panel for cover."

As they retreated, two more shots rang out. This time, Victoria clearly heard the characteristic whistle of the bullets as they passed within inches of her skull.

Using all his past military experience, John tried to determine where the shots might have come from. Lifting his head over the partition that protected them, he saw the silhouette of their attacker.

Two more shots rang out.

"I spotted someone above us, a little farther away. He must have come in through the ventilation."

"What are we going to do?" Victoria asked, worried. "We're pinned down."

With a quick, precise glance, John took stock of what he had at hand. Only a wrench, no doubt forgotten by the maintenance crews, lay to his left.

"If I could get to the valve on that hot water pipe over there, it would be a good diversion," John said, "but I've only got one shot."

"Leave it to me, John," Victoria cut in. "I'm the darts champion of New Eldorado City. I'm no stranger to precision shots."

John hesitated for a second. Two more shots rang out.

"Unbeaten for four years," Victoria insisted, her green eyes fixed on him.

"Yes, all right. Go ahead—but be ready to run for the stairs. We don't have much time."

John still wondered why he'd agreed so quickly.

"I don't plan on staying long," Victoria nodded.

Still crouched, Victoria got into position. She counted down three seconds in her head, focusing all her attention on the target. Holding her breath, she threw the wrench with all her strength.

Turning on itself, the tool reached its target with rare precision, and the valve was released from its casing. At the same moment, a jet of steam shot out of the pipe, obscuring John and Victoria from their attacker.

"Let's go!" John shouted, rising to his feet with a connoisseur's appreciation of the beauty of the gesture.

They both ran for the nearby stairs, and Victoria took the lead, tumbling down them four at a time. John looked up to see the gunman's face, but he was already gone.

At the bottom of the stairs, they took the first available exit to get out of the hallways.

"Let's hurry and get the Navigon to the Naviport. I don't think whoever he is is going to stay there."

In the Navigon that took them to the shuttle, Victoria couldn't help but comment on the situation. She mentioned Buba, their misadventure the night before, and the fact that it could only be Kellnik who had found them and was now after their lives.

Listening with one ear, John analysed the situation. Victoria continued her story, ignoring Bedford's plea for discretion. She left no stone unturned—no doubt exhilarated by the adrenaline still coursing through her system.

A few minutes later, they arrived at the Naviport.

"I'd like to bring you back to reality, Victoria. I don't think it's safe for either of us on the station. I'll tell you more aboard the shuttle, but if I'm not mistaken, we're both in danger. I'll tell Bedford I'm coming with you and change our flight plan to be on the safe side. I won't be long."

Victoria waited by the shuttle and scanned the area, hoping not to attract the attention of Kellnik or any of his companions. Only a mechanic was busy preparing the shuttle for launch.

A few minutes later, Victoria and John boarded the shuttle back to Earth.

Once clear of the runway, John made a 90-degree turn to skirt the station for a while. Victoria took the opportunity to continue the conversation. She needed to know what John thought.

"You said you'd give me an explanation once we were on board," Victoria began.

John pressed a series of buttons, and after a brief computer announcement—"Autopilot engaged"—he turned to her and spoke.

"Well, here's what I think. We've both been targeted in the corridors, and it's not the work of your Buba Kellnik."

Victoria was a little surprised by such a statement, but she looked forward to hearing more.

"We agree that our attacker's main objective was to eliminate you. If he'd wanted to attack me, he would have waited until you were gone."

Victoria nodded, one eyebrow raised—clearly intrigued.

"Secondly, the false failure of the Navigon and the place where we were attacked make me think the attacker knows me personally and knows the station perfectly. He knew that in the case of a malfunction, I'd go through the corridors instead of turning back.

Our attacker anticipated my actions too well for him to have only wanted to attack you."

"Why do you think he's after you too?" Victoria asked. "Sure, he guessed you'd come through the corridors, but that doesn't mean he wanted to take it out on you."

"If our attacker knows me so well, I must also know him—at least by sight. At the very least, I'm an inconvenient witness who needs to be eliminated. Since it's certain that I'll be able to identify him, I'm de facto in his line of fire."

"And what about Buba?"

"Once again, the location of the attack leads me to conclude that the assailant has excellent local knowledge. From what you've told me about Kellnik, I don't think he has the knowledge or connections to organise this kind of trap."

"However, what I heard on Earth made me think they were well organised," Victoria replied. "But do you have any idea who our attacker is?"

John paused for a moment.

"I have no idea—which is why I've changed our flight plan. I want to take you to a friend who might be able to shed some light on our case."

John took over the manual controls to steer away from the station and towards Earth, and Victoria sank back into her chair. She had the distinct impression that John was taking the blame. He had no idea who had attacked them, and that seemed to upset him greatly.

No sooner had John left the station's orbit than the shuttle was shaken violently.

"What now?" Victoria worried.

"I don't know, but it came from behind," John said, fiddling with his dashboard. "I think another shuttle just tried to ram us. It's probably our attackers—they clearly have a mind of their own."

"Are you kidding? They can't do that, I'm going to..."

Victoria couldn't finish her sentence as the ramming continued. The shuttle was being jolted from all sides, and she found it hard not to be thrown from her seat.

"Oh, oh!" shouted John as he tried various manoeuvres to lose his pursuer.

"What do you mean, 'Oh, oh'? I don't like that 'Oh, oh' at all."

"Neither do I," replied John. "I'm afraid we've been hit."

"Better and better. I'm so glad you came; I feel much safer now."

"Please, Victoria, let me concentrate. Your sarcasm doesn't help me at all."

Two new impacts shook the shuttle, harder than the last.

"Shit. This time we're losing fuel. This is not good—not good at all," John muttered to himself.

Suddenly, the blows stopped.

"Are they gone? Are they gone?" asked Victoria.

"They're gone because their job is done."

"What do you mean by that?"

"By ramming us, they've managed to create a plasma leak, and with what we're losing, we'll never reach the cow floor—or at least not gently. Once the plasma runs out, the engines will overheat, and the shuttle will explode," John replied coolly.

"Given your calm, I assume you have a plan?"

John continued manipulating nearly every button he could reach. Several dials began flashing at once.

"Have you ever jumped with a parachute?" he asked, surprisingly relieved.

"You're lucky," Victoria replied. "My father was an experienced skydiver. He always told me it would come in handy one day."

John, who had expected surprise, was in turn surprised by her composure.

"Go to the bottom of the cabin—in the upper compartment— you'll find the parachutes. Put one on and give me another. Hurry, we've only got a few seconds."

Victoria complied, while John entered one or two more commands into the onboard computer, which was now flashing like Christmas lights.

Then John stood and joined Victoria near the airlock.

"Ready to go?"

Victoria looked briefly into John's eyes, as if to confirm she understood.

"Ready," she replied.

John grabbed the ejection handle of the airlock.

"Given our speed, it's going to be quite violent," John said. "Hold your breath as long as you can—your chute will open automatically."

Victoria nodded and took a deep breath. John pulled the lever.

The airlock exploded in a shower of sparks, and the pressure difference between the inside and outside of the cabin created a powerful draft that instantly swept them both out of the shuttle.

Under the force of the blast, Victoria lost all sense of direction for a few seconds. When she regained her bearings, she saw John struggling to steady himself. A little higher up, the shuttle was spinning on its axis. Victoria fell to Earth in an uncontrolled free fall, keeping her eyes fixed on John as a reference point.

A moment later, there was a huge explosion. She looked away—

the shuttle had just exploded in a plume of blue light, caused by what remained of the plasma in the power conduits.

Debris from the wreckage quickly caught up with them, and both John and Victoria feared being struck. John tried in vain to grab Victoria and pull her clear.

Like a boxing glove thrown by Mike Tyson at the height of his powers, a piece of debris from one of the shuttle's seats collided with John's head. Stunned but not knocked unconscious, John was forced to descend, hoping to avoid being caught in the shuttle's aftermath.

John and Victoria's free fall seemed endless. After many long minutes, their parachutes opened almost in unison. They landed a few feet apart on a deserted beach.

"Thank God we're safe," John said, collapsing to the ground.

Victoria barely had time to respond before she too collapsed.

"Thanks, Dad."

Chapter Four
I Won't Let Them

That afternoon, Archi Mac Dugan had an appointment with Gerald Bedford to report his findings on the control of the facilities under his responsibility.

Bedford had been waiting for Mac Dugan to arrive for nearly a quarter of an hour.

"Berenice, could you come in here, please?" Bedford said through the half-open door of his office.

"Yes, sir," replied his secretary, arriving in the office almost immediately.

"Do you know where Mac Dugan is? He's running late."

"I don't know, sir. He didn't call to cancel."

"Well, call Mr Desmond. He should be home by now."

"I'm sorry, sir. I didn't see Mr Mac Dugan arrive, and I tried to call Mr Desmond, but he's not available either."

"So there's no one at his post on this station," Bedford remarked exasperatedly. "Desmond told me he was taking Miss Palmers back to Earth for some obscure security reason, but he should be back by now. As for Mac Dugan, I want him to give me a full report on these energy spikes that are affecting transmissions to Earth."

"I'll call the docks to see if the shuttle has returned," Berenice said.

"I'm going to see if Mac Dugan is in his office. I want him to explain to me, face to face, why he hasn't deigned to answer my summons. Call me there if you hear anything."

"Yes, sir."

Meanwhile, the elevator in Little California's one-legged module unloaded its daily batch of commuters. Among the passengers entering the station, Buba Kellnik and his two accomplices had managed to blend in with the work crews, using fake Health Inspector cards that gave them access to just about every part of the station without arousing suspicion.

"Gentlemen, you know what we've got to do," Buba said to his two companions, who nodded in agreement. "Let's get going—our destination is only a stone's throw from here. Follow me."

On the way to Mac Dugan's office, Gerald Bedford thought back to his conversation with Victoria Palmers. One question kept coming back to him: how in the world could the energy spikes turn into such intense heatwaves on Earth?

As Station Manager, he knew that the protocols for energy transfer were very strict. In the event of repeated failures, the computers would have automatically taken steps to limit the amount of energy being transferred to prevent power surges.

Only human intervention could have caused these heatwaves.

Unlikely as it may have seemed, the person best placed to carry out this kind of manipulation was Mac Dugan. Ever since the assassination attempt, his behaviour had been suspicious. According to Bedford, Mac Dugan should have found the source of the energy spikes long ago. He wanted to be sure before he told John. He was his best friend, and if his fears were justified, such a revelation would be disastrous for the station's stability.

Arriving at Mac Dugan's office, Bedford entered unannounced, hoping to surprise him and gain the upper hand.

But the surprise was of a different nature. As soon as he entered, Bedford realised the office had been ransacked. The entire room was in disarray—though not entirely unlike Archi's usual habits. The safe had been opened, and the filing cabinets emptied of their most sensitive contents.

Given the state of the place, Bedford began to doubt Mac Dugan's involvement. One thing was certain: the energy spikes were no longer random, and the possibility that Earth was in danger seemed increasingly likely.

In the course of his inspection, Bedford's eyes fell on a patch of ground near the office door. Bending down for a closer look, he realised it was a stain of prepanol—a chemical product found exclusively on the station's shuttles.

While Bedford puzzled over how it might have got there, he felt compelled to report the matter to his Chief of Security. John Desmond would no doubt have an idea about Mac Dugan's possible involvement and, with any luck, be able to exonerate him. Perhaps he'd also be able to explain how it had been so easy to break into a secure area.

Just as Bedford was about to head back to his office, a sharp pain shot through his skull. Groggily, he barely had time to run a hand through his hair and feel the blood before collapsing onto the floor of Mac Dugan's office.

Three men stood behind him, apparently satisfied they had found what they were looking for.

"I told you not to hit him too hard," Buba Kellnik said to one of his accomplices. "I hope you didn't kill him. We need him alive. According to our informant," he added, "this Mac Dugan is behind it all. Let's get him to the right place."

At the same time, Victoria came to her senses on the beach of Fregola.

"How are you?" John said as he leaned over her.

"I've had better days. Haven't you?" replied Victoria.

"Aside from the debris that knocked me out when I landed, I'm fine."

"Before I woke you, I took a look around to determine our position."

"So where are we?"

"I think we're on the beach at Fregola—and we're lucky."

"Ah, you think so?" Victoria cut in. "Fregola? Never heard of it. There's not a soul around; we're alone, and the next town must be hundreds of miles away."

"Stop grumbling," John said with a slight smile. "I told you I'd changed our flight plan to visit a friend. Well—he's a crazy computer scientist who lives nearby. It's just a few miles north. I thought I'd take you straight there by shuttle, but this beach is worth a look, isn't it?"

"A computer scientist who's a bit crazy," Victoria pointed out. "You're sure that's appropriate in our situation?"

"He's a very nice guy, you'll see. And his computer knowledge will help us," John replied, before setting off.

After a half-hour walk along the only road bordering the beach, John and Victoria came upon a blockhouse from the Factional War. More than just a blockhouse, it was an advanced observation post and communications relay. This concrete tower, some 70 feet in diameter and as tall as a three-storey building, was anchored at the base of a cliff overlooking the entire beach. The upper part was a dome made entirely of beranium glass, giving the structure an unreal appearance. The contrast between the raw concrete and the beranium—a semi-transparent material depending on the angle from which it was viewed—offered a very particular spectacle and, from inside, a 360° view of the surrounding area.

"Is this where we're going?" asked Victoria, a little surprised by the appearance of the building.

"Yes. Interesting, isn't it?" John replied. "It gives you an idea of the character I'm about to introduce."

"A sci-fi fan," Victoria surmised. "This building looks like R2-D2 with his arms removed."

"An R2-D2?" asked John.

"Yes, it's a famous little robot from the 20th century."

"I know what it is," John interrupted, "but I'm surprised you do too." John's gaze lingered on Victoria. That reference to the 20th century seemed to make her even more attractive to him.

When they reached the foot of the building, its colossal nature became fully apparent. The military imprint of the place was tangible. John flipped a switch that seemed to act as the doorbell. The massive, partially rusted steel door began to glow in the centre. A man—visibly busy—materialised on the screen that had just appeared.

"I didn't order anything. Go away," the man said, not bothering to raise his head.

"Jacky, it's Johnny. I need to see you."

"Desmond, is that you?" he replied, raising his head. His expression changed and suddenly became radiant. "Yes, it is you… and you seem to be in good company," he added, rubbing his hands together. The screen went blank.

Victoria, who had been in the background, couldn't help but speak up.

"He seems nice, but are you sure he'll be able to help us?"

"I'm sure, Victoria. But if I may say so—we should pretend to be together. Otherwise, he won't let you go."

"Together?" Victoria replied. "You mean..."

"Yes. Jacky is a lovely boy, but he's an original—and women are a big part of that originality."

"I see," said Victoria, a little annoyed at being presented with a fait accompli. "And shall I call you darling, or my love?"

"Let's keep it simple. But we'll need to be on first-name terms. I just hope he doesn't ask us to kiss."

"Sorry..."

Victoria didn't have time to finish her sentence when the door swung open.

"Shh," John said with an amused look. "He's coming."

Jacky Collman was a quirky man who lived and breathed his passion. Of average height and often scruffy-looking, he always wore a pair of round glasses that he could have easily done without, but which gave him the necessary sense of belonging to the world he loved—computers. Without what you might call a disguise, Jacky Collman had a certain charm that he regularly abused with the ladies.

"John, I'm delighted to see you," said Jacky. "And I see you're not here alone. Please, come in. Make yourselves at home."

John and Victoria entered the building, and the large door closed behind them.

They followed Jacky down a long, dark, dimly lit corridor to a large circular room in the centre of the building. Around the edge of the room was a battery of obsolete-looking computers that must have been used during the Factional War. The military atmosphere of the time had been perfectly preserved. The room had no windows; the only source of natural light came from the centre of the room via a double circular metal staircase leading to the observatory. Only one part of the room stood out. Jacky had set up his study there, and the modernity of the space stood in stark contrast to the coldness of the rest.

"So tell me, what's become of you? It's been a while since I've heard from you or Archi," Jacky said. "But first of all, don't keep me in the dark. You know I love it when you come in good company." Jacky's gaze undressed Victoria almost as surely as if he'd used his hands.

"This is Victoria Palmers."

"Nice to meet you," Victoria tried.

"And you're together?" Jacky said to John, without taking his eyes off Victoria.

"Yes, it's been three years," John replied quickly. "Hasn't it, darling?"

"Yes, three years," Victoria confirmed, raising her eyebrows.

Jacky watched the reactions of his two guests carefully.

"I've come to you to help us test a theory," John said.

"Can you kiss?" Jacky asked, turning back to the computers that needed his attention.

Victoria exclaimed, almost choking.

John took advantage of Jacky's momentary inattention to lean over to Victoria and whisper in her ear.

"I warned you—women are his guilty pleasure. If we don't comply, he won't let you go, and we won't get anything out of him. Given our situation, we need answers. Think of it as an act of God."

"You've got some good ones," Victoria replied.

"John, I know you, my friend," Jacky said, leaving his console. "You've done this to me before, and I'm not going to be fooled a second time—unless there's even the slightest chance of getting to know her better..."

"Very well," John interrupted, cutting the conversation short.

Victoria said nothing, but she was seething inside that she'd let herself fall into this trap.

"Just one kiss," John continued.

"A kiss is all I ask," Jacky agreed. "You know, that's how I judge a couple."

John and Victoria turned to face each other. Victoria smiled superficially but decided to play along. After all, she reassured herself, this cinematic kiss could mean nothing.

As their faces slowly approached, Victoria felt more tense than ever. But she reminded herself she had no reason to be stressed by this simple game. Their lips met with such gentleness that she didn't immediately realise their movie-theatre kiss had turned into a real one.

In an instant, all her tension dissolved, and Victoria tightened her embrace around John. She forgot where she was and let herself be carried away in a languorous kiss.

For his part, John's feeling was unsettling at first. He hadn't kissed anyone since Isabella's death, and the pleasure he felt made him feel guilty. But soon, the sensuality of Victoria's kiss enveloped his mind and erased all remorse.

They were interrupted only by Jacky's applause, which brought them both back to reality. John and Victoria realised that something had happened, and for a moment, they could hardly take their eyes off each other.

"Well done," said Jacky, who couldn't stop applauding as he bounced up and down in his chair. "I didn't believe for a moment in your story as a couple, but it's clear that after three years, you still love each other as much as on the first day. It reminds me of the glory days of the Three Arrows—but last time, you were less convincing."

"The Three Arrows? The last time?" Victoria wondered, trying to regain her composure.

"Jacky, Archi and Johnny—that was the Three Arrows," Jacky continued, "and our motto was 'Straight as an arrow, even after three bottles of whisky.'"

"We were young. That's all in the past," John tried to conclude.

"But I'm interested, darling," Victoria said, thinking she'd got her revenge.

"Very good," Jacky continued. "It happened during our service in the army. We were as close as the fingers of one hand. We did the four hundred and one together, and even though we went our separate ways, we always stayed close. Anyway, one night when we'd had too much to drink—no doubt to perfect our motto—John got it into his head to make me believe the girl I was after was with him. And as you've just seen, my technique for finding out the truth is simple but effective."

"Indeed, I agree that it's very effective," Victoria added, still moved.

"Only this time," Jacky continued, "the girl was even drunker than we were, and the moment John started to kiss her, she fell into an ethyl coma. It was impossible to revive her. Archi and I were bent over, watching John stagger around, trying in vain to wake her up—'My love, kiss me, kiss me, kiss me,'" he repeated, pushing his lips forward and glassing his eyes over.

John began to blush like a child caught in the act. Victoria was pleased to see him so embarrassed. *He must be feeling the same embarrassment I felt earlier,* she thought. She couldn't help but burst out laughing as she imagined the scene, and Jacky, caught up in Victoria's infectious laughter, laughed along with her.

"Yes, very funny," John said. "But now that you've reminded me of that unforgettable story, perhaps you can show us your real talent and try to help us."

"I'm listening, Johnny."

John and Victoria explained the facts in detail. The last 24 hours had been eventful, and the theory Victoria had explained to Bedford about overloads during energy transfers to Earth was of great interest to Jacky.

"If I understand you both correctly, you think you've uncovered a conspiracy to create natural disasters—but artificially."

"That doesn't sound very serious," Victoria said.

"On the contrary," Jacky replied. "I think your theory is very interesting. Using one-legged modules to create heat waves during energy transfer and destabilise the climate is brilliant... but impossible."

"Impossible?" said Victoria.

"Because on the station," Jacky continued, "the one-legged modules are controlled by different governments. That's impossible. On Earth, it would have taken a war that could have wiped out humanity for all the governments to agree and create Stargraber. I don't see how such a conspiracy could be organised on an international level. The interests of some rarely coincide with those of others.

"On the other hand, and from what you're telling me, Victoria, in order for heat waves to have a significant effect on the global climate, every module surrounding the Earth would have to be used in a coordinated manner, and their actions synchronised to achieve a result. That would be like hacking the entire station. Well, I'll say it again: impossible! Each DPT responsible for modules uses its own computer system. A heresy—but as I said, the interests of some... A real mess. Even when I try to hack into a small part of the station, I have a hard time finding my way around. So, to think that someone could synchronise everything from a single workstation is, well, impossible!"

"But we haven't been dreaming for the last 24 hours," John said. "Victoria overheard a conversation about taking over one of the station's one-legged modules. The power spikes are real too—not to mention the sound of the bullets passing near your head."

"I'm not questioning the fact that someone has a grudge against Victoria. But with the information you've given me, I can't subscribe to the conspiracy theory, at least not in this form. There are far too many variables to consider for such an intervention to be possible."

"Can you do a background check on Buba Kellnik?" asked Victoria.

"Wait and see," Jacky replied, turning back to his screens.

Jacky's search had barely begun when his multiple screens already displayed a plethora of answers.

"I don't see anything unusual about this man," Jacky said, consulting his screens. "He owns half of New Eldorado City, but apparently, he's not into anything particularly shady."

Victoria seemed distraught that Jacky couldn't find anything on Buba. *There must be something,* she thought.

At that moment, Jacky stopped. John, who knew him well, noticed immediately.

"What is it?" asked John.

"I'm not sure," Jacky replied. "I found a strange connection. Hang on, I'll check it out."

As soon as he clicked on the link, all of Jacky's computers began flashing at once. Jacky then seemed to go into an almost frenetic dance, tapping his keyboard and clicking his mouse with a dexterity that would have made a magician jealous.

Victoria gave John a quizzical look. She was amazed to see anyone using a keyboard and mouse in those days. As far as she was concerned, Jacky was some kind of happy, enlightened man.

"Someone's trying to infiltrate my system," he said between mouse clicks. "I've seen you," he continued, almost jokingly, "but I've got you. Now it's my turn to infiltrate. My installation may seem outdated, but I'm on the cutting edge of technology. I don't know who your Buba is, but he is extremely well-protected. I'm going to run a programme or two of my own. We'll see if his protection system can withstand me."

Victoria seemed to regain hope. Jacky had obviously stumbled upon something important. Now she was sure she wasn't crazy. Lost in thought, she blurted out that last thought aloud.

"I never said you were crazy, darling," John replied mechanically.

Victoria paused before answering, realising that her thoughts were no longer truly her own.

"Thank you for your support, my love, but the last 24 hours have made me think otherwise."

John and Victoria exchanged a knowing look, telling each other that they weren't such bad actors after all—even if Jacky was far too busy to pay attention to their performance.

"Now I've got something," he said, staring at his screens. "I managed to counter their attack, but it wasn't from Buba Kellnik. As

I study the source code, it's easy to see that your target is already heavily guarded. I can't tell you who's behind this, but I've been able to identify two very different sources. One at the station, the other in New Albuquerque. I can't pinpoint the first, but if you want, I can give you an address for the second."

"I'm listening," said John.

"The address is 43 General Carol Avenue, right in the centre of New Albuquerque. I'll upload a map to your Gcom."

"Don't bother," John replied. "I know exactly where it is."

"An official building?" asked Victoria.

"No, it's an office building near me," said John, not knowing what to think.

"But... I thought you lived at the station," Jacky continued.

"That's where I live now. But this is where I lived before the accident." In an instant, John remembered his former life. But most painfully, he remembered the accident that had changed it forever.

Victoria sensed the discomfort and tried to distract him.

"I know it's hard," she said, "but look on the bright side. At least we know where to look for answers."

John remained silent and stepped aside for a moment. Victoria tried to follow, but Jacky stopped her, signalling with his eyes that she should give John a moment. She complied, feeling helpless in the face of his quiet grief. True, they were playing a role in front of

Jacky, but the casual kiss they had shared earlier made her feel that they were already closer than she'd expected.

"Does Buba Kellnik have any special connection to this address?" Victoria asked Jacky.

"Hang on, I'm looking... No, I don't see anything. But the offices have been empty for years."

Jacky brought up the structure of the building on his screen. Each room appeared with all its associated information. None of the data connected Buba Kellnik to the address.

"Jacky, could you be more specific?" Victoria insisted. "If we knew where the information being exchanged with the station was coming from, it would make our task much easier."

Despite the memories still too vivid, John returned, not wanting to miss any developments. This time, Victoria took his hand, a silent gesture that showed him his pain meant something to her. John gave a faint nod, indicating he appreciated her support.

"Triangulating the signal is almost impossible," said Jacky. "Unless the target is actively transmitting, I can't be more accurate than ground level. Their signal is very well disguised. They've mixed it in with standard Gcom traffic. If you weren't paying attention, you'd think it was just a simple conversation between a grandmother and her grandson.

"Their mistake was trying to find out if someone was looking for information about Buba Kellnik—and who. With a normal person, their intrusion would probably have gone unnoticed. But they found me, and I won't let them go."

"I'm listening, Jacky. Tell us what floor it is," said John.

"If you're looking for answers to your questions, I strongly suggest you look at the top floor."

Victoria and Jacky both turned to see John's reaction. His expression hardened. His brows furrowed. Determination settled in.

"Is there any way to know who the current owner is?" asked John.

"No, I'm sorry, Johnny. Although it seems impossible these days, the owner is anonymous. But this isn't the only building like that. In your old building, adjacent to those offices, there are two other apartments in the same situation—your old apartment and the one on the third floor. Neither has a registered owner. Don't tell me you know the person who lives there."

"Not exactly," John replied. "But I know very well who lived there when I was there."

"But yes—I'm stupid," said Jacky. "Archi! It's obvious. I remember when we finished school, you and Archi were inseparable. I wonder if you two didn't even consider getting a flat together."

"Yes, you're absolutely right, Jacky," said John with a half-smile. "That's how I ended up with that huge penthouse. We bought it together at first, but it didn't take us three months to realise that military life had absolutely nothing to do with civilian life. It was like a couple who get married on impulse and gradually realise they're not meant to live together."

"I hope you're not going to do that to me," Victoria interrupted. "Now I understand why you're keen to keep your bachelor pad on the station."

"I thought you lived together 24 hours a day," Jacky said. "There might be an opening—you never know."

As Victoria tried to make Jacky understand that there would *never* be an opening for him, John was more concerned with why the two historically linked apartments now both had anonymous owners.

Gathering his memories, he recalled that, distraught after Isabella's disappearance, he had entrusted Archi with selling his apartment so he could move to Stargraber. To whom had Archi sold it? At the time, John had only been interested in the proceeds and hadn't asked any questions. Archi hadn't offered details either.

"Victoria," John said, snapping out of his thoughts, "we have to go to Albuquerque. I think we'll find the beginnings of an answer there."

"I don't mind, John," Victoria replied, "but what about Buba Kellnik? He chased me all over New Eldorado City, and he's probably the one who tracked us to the station. We can't just drop that lead."

"We're not dropping it, Victoria. But *he's* the one who's led us to my old apartment. I'm sure that when we get there, we'll find out why he's after you."

In the face of John's determination, Victoria told herself that her experience as an investigator at the station would probably lead them in the right direction. Buba Kellnik could wait; she felt that whatever happened, their fates were now intertwined—probably more for the worse than the better.

"There's just one problem," John said. "I wonder how we're going to get to Albuquerque."

"May I ask how you got here?" asked Jacky.

"Quite simply, in a shuttle that exploded in mid-air," Victoria replied, clearly proud of her answer.

"I see," Jacky said, wondering whether Victoria was serious. "I think I've got just the thing for you. It's not first-hand, but it'll get you where you need to go. Grab your things and follow me to the garage."

After descending a few steps, they found themselves in the basement, in a completely dark room. Jacky searched for the switch for a moment before letting John and Victoria discover their new means of transport.

"Well, what do you think?" Jacky said. "Isn't it great?"

John and Victoria were stunned. They were looking at what was probably the last of the Harley-Davidsons. The chrome had not been maintained in years, but it looked perfectly functional. A passion for vintage transport was just one of the many things that brought the two men together. It was a gorgeous late 21st-century Fatboy—one of the brand's final productions before it was shut down by competition from automated vehicles.

"I see you haven't changed," said John, examining the beast from every angle. "You're still riding on two wheels, and I wonder when you'll finally decide to ride on four."

"We've had this conversation before, and my main point still stands: man started on all fours and ended up on two legs."

Victoria, for her part, was less enthusiastic about the prospect of riding several hundred miles astride a machine whose only protection was a rudimentary braking system and a helmet. Plus, the thickness of the saddle was more like an overcooked steak than a Pullman lounge chair.

"I added two extra bladders to the saddlebags," said Jacky. "You should have no trouble getting to Albuquerque. Don't forget to contact me when you get there. If you can get me access to their communications network, I can probably tell you where on the station they're broadcasting from."

Meanwhile, three men accompanied by a stretcher took the elevators from the one-legged module to Earth. Thanks to their disguise as health inspectors, Buba Kellnik and his accomplices were free to evacuate their prisoner to Earth, where they could interrogate him without risk of disturbance.

Arriving in New Eldorado City, Kellnik decided to take his prisoner to an underground shelter in one of the galleries he still owned.

"We'll be safe here," Buba Kellnik told his accomplices. "If we don't get the answers we want and the interrogation gets harder, no one will hear him scream."

Gradually, Gerald Bedford awoke from his sedated sleep. He was locked in a side room of an underground shelter dug into the rock. As he slowly regained consciousness, his first instinct was to call for help. Immediately, the rattling wooden door opened with a distinctive creak. A man—whose silhouette he could only just make out—stood in the doorway.

"Where am I?" muttered Bedford. "Who the hell are you? What do you want from me?"

"I see you're awake," said the apparently plump man. "That's very good, but please be quiet. I'll come and get you in a few minutes. And don't scream. Apart from losing your voice, no one will hear you."

"At least tell me where I am," Bedford said, hoping to start a conversation.

"You'll find out soon enough. Shut up and be quiet. I wouldn't advise you to make me angry."

Once the door was closed, Bedford tried to calm himself and think about why he'd been brought there. His position of responsibility within the station made him a public figure, but he couldn't understand why anyone would want to kidnap him.

Suddenly, the activity Bedford perceived behind the door seemed to intensify. Trying to understand what was going on, he moved closer and pressed his ear to it. The cave was so loud that Bedford could only hear an incomprehensible din. Nevertheless, his experience as a boss—accustomed to reading the mood of colleagues by the tone of a corridor conversation—convinced him he recognised the tension of an argument.

This was my chance, he thought. A good fight could save the day. The tone was still rising. They'll probably all kill each other, Bedford continued to hope.

He couldn't have been more right. Amidst the clatter of words, he recognised the distinct sound of a particle weapon. Capable of disintegrating a human being, these weapons of faction warfare had been banned from American territory. They had been deemed inhumane by Congress, who no doubt preferred their citizens to continue killing each other with more civilised guns.

In an instant, he felt panic overtake him. Nevertheless, he decided to hide in one of the cracks in the wall. Since the room was completely dark, he thought he might have a chance. His heart rate now soared past 160.

A few minutes later, the cave was quiet again. Now he would find out whether all his hard work in the gym had caused him to lose enough stomach to blend into the wall.

The door opened with a bang, no doubt kicked in by one of his attackers. The beam of a flashlight swept across the room. Bedford's heart rate must have exceeded 190. In a last-ditch effort, he held his breath to further flatten his silhouette.

After what seemed like an eternity, the light disappeared.

Bedford was relieved, but curious to know what had happened. He slowly approached the half-open door. The adjoining room was virtually empty—furnished only with an overturned, battered table, a few chairs, and an old, scuffed sideboard. Obviously, his captors and their assailants had all left.

As he headed for the door, Bedford recoiled. He hadn't seen the body of a man hidden by the table he'd just walked around. After checking his pulse, he decided to venture further into the gallery toward a point of light that seemed to indicate an exit.

Glancing around to make sure he was alone, Gerald Bedford moved forward as cautiously as possible. After a few dozen feet, he finally caught sight of what appeared to be daylight.

But his relief was short-lived. Several men stood guard at the entrance to the underground passageway. Bedford stepped back and waited for long minutes, hoping they would leave. There was another tunnel to the right, but not knowing where it led, it seemed even more dangerous.

Disappointed, he decided to retrace his steps to the shelter and look for another solution. A thorough search of the room revealed only a flashlight with a dying battery.

He sat on one of the rickety chairs, lifted the table, and rapped his forehead several times against it. His situation seemed truly desperate.

New noises echoed in the adjacent corridor. Lost and at a loss for what to do, Bedford decided to investigate. He had barely stepped through the door of the shelter when he saw dozens of miners coming up from deep underground.

He knew he wouldn't get a second chance. Plucking up the courage to undress the corpse that had kept him company, he donned the jumpsuit and helmet and joined the stream of workers. As he approached the exit, the guards were still in place.

He tucked his head into his shoulders, pulled the helmet down tighter, and prayed that no one would recognise him. The lookouts, who were only concerned with themselves, continued talking as the miners passed.

Bedford listened—and was stunned by what he heard.

I can't have heard right, he thought. It just can't be. Archi Mac Dugan couldn't be behind my kidnapping. Yet I clearly heard his name spoken just now.

Confused and perplexed, Gerald Bedford realised that there was only one person he could talk to about all of this. He had to find John Desmond as soon as possible and warn him that Archi, if not responsible for all of this, must know what was going on. His name was mentioned far too often to be a coincidence.

Knowing that his attackers were well acquainted with New Eldorado City, he made his way to the megalopolis of Albuquerque, where, lost in the crowd, he might have a chance to go unnoticed. Anonymous, it would probably be the only place where he would feel out of reach of his pursuers.

John and Victoria arrived in Albuquerque in the early evening. They were still about 50 km from the outskirts of the city, but the megalopolis already loomed majestically above them. The city was surrounded by towering buildings that seemed to form an impenetrable barrier. Only the incessant ballet of flycars seemed able to pass between these monsters of concrete and steel. The largest of them seemed directly connected to the stars, and from a certain angle, the façades of some of them, dimly lit and adorned with mirrors, reflected the celestial vault, accentuating the disproportionate size of the city.

The city was one of the first new megacities to be created with a completely redesigned architecture. In fact, all skyscrapers had been relegated to the outskirts. They were built to allow light into the heart of the city despite their gigantic size. The historic centre now consisted of small buildings no higher than three storeys. The city seemed surrounded by gigantic monoliths. As a result, the centre of this megalopolis of nearly 45 million people had the feel of a resort town.

The city centre was entirely dedicated to tourism and the preservation of architectural heritage. As for the outskirts, each building was designed as a city in itself. In each building, there were botanical gardens where you could grow plants and food or just relax. There were also shops, business centres, schools, churches, museums – in short, everything that makes up a neighbourhood. All of this had been put in place to minimise the need for residents to travel and thus reduce inconvenience. As a result, traffic congestion was virtually non-existent, and telecommuting was booming.

As they approached the first buildings surrounding the city, known as the Great Barrier, night fell, and each building revealed a little more of its amazing structure. One of the most remarkable features was the hanging gardens in the centre of the buildings, which let in light during the day but seemed to float in the middle of the structure at night. Victoria, who hadn't left New Eldorado City for a long time, was amazed, as she always was when she came to one of these megacities.

After crossing the Great Barrier, John, who did more driving than flying, headed for the centre of the city. Though a gigantic megalopolis, it seemed empty at dusk, almost ghostly. Only a few tourists strolled through the business districts. Neighbourhood life had been replaced by building life over time. Since people could find everything on-site, they tended to stay at home.

"We need to find a hotel for the night," he told Victoria through the Gcom in his helmet.

"I'll let you choose, since I've no idea where we're going," Victoria answered.

"I know a very good one, just a stone's throw from my old address. If the owner hasn't changed, we'll be very well received."

Indeed, after a few minutes' drive through the perfectly manicured streets of downtown, they arrived at a hacienda-shaped hotel that was eerily reminiscent of the Mexican saloons of yesteryear. The place didn't stand out from its surroundings. The entire downtown had been deliberately preserved as a late 20th-century New Mexico town and was the pride of its residents. Only the locals didn't live there, because the downtown was primarily for show and tourists.

Nothing had been forgotten: neither the yellow ochre walls nor the exposed beams, and above all, they had managed to preserve the typical atmosphere of a town with a central square. Each district had its own heart, around which the lives of its inhabitants revolved. Tourists were enchanted by what was probably the most historically significant place in the United States. The blend of classicism and modernity gave New Albuquerque a special place in American history.

After a romantic dinner on one of the hotel's rooftops, John and Victoria agreed it was time to recharge their batteries. The next day would be intense. In their respective rooms, both tried to recall past events without understanding what was happening to them.

John felt like he was alive again: he hadn't had a drop to drink in 24 hours and was once again experiencing feelings he never thought he had the right to feel. His life on the station seemed to be in danger, but the feeling of adrenaline coursing through his veins was a lifesaver. However, this feeling of well-being was counterbalanced by the fact that Archi's name came up all too often in this affair.

The same disturbing feelings ran through Victoria's mind. What should she make of that kiss? Even if it wasn't real, she was convinced that something deeper had happened. Yet neither she nor John had broached the subject at dinner.

Who was after her life? What would they find tomorrow in the offices adjacent to John's apartment? Why would people want to create some kind of global catastrophe?

"No, they won't," Victoria muttered before falling asleep. "I won't let them."

Chapter Five

I Hate Him Already

The next day, after a short, restless night, John and Victoria took the Fatboy back to John's old apartment.

"I did a lot of thinking last night," Victoria said. "Some things don't add up. If, as Jacky says, we can't synchronise the one-legged modules to create larger heat waves, then my theory of a worldwide attack is wrong."

"Yeah, I've been thinking about that too," John said. "But maybe they're after something else."

"I agree, but if that's the case, we have another problem. Any manipulation of the power transfer modules can only be done with the approval of the DPT. And if I'm not mistaken, the DPT is your friend, Archi Mac Dugan."

"Everything you say is true. I can't believe that Archi has anything to do with sabotage. What I do believe is that he may be the victim of blackmail. In that case, we need to get in touch with him..."

The call had just ended. Victoria checked her headset in vain. After a few minutes of silence, communication was restored.

"What happened?" asked Victoria.

"I just got a strange call," John replied. "It was Gerald Bedford. He's here on Earth, in New Albuquerque. He told me the most incredible story. He'd been kidnapped and managed to escape. I arranged to meet him outside my old apartment."

"This case is definitely taking a turn I don't like."

Arriving at 43 Rue du Général Carol, John and Victoria immediately saw Gerald Bedford. He was obviously very nervous and kept scanning his surroundings.

"It's Bedford," John said. "Come on, Victoria, let's find him."

"John, I'm glad to see you," said Bedford, visibly relieved. "I thought my last hour had come."

"Tell me what happened to you," John replied. "If there's anything we can do to help, we'd be glad to."

"In short, I can tell you that I was kidnapped by a pot-bellied man who was himself the victim of a heavily armed assailant. It was only their scuffle that allowed me to escape, otherwise I'd probably still be under heavy interrogation. I don't know why or who kidnapped me."

"It's Buba Kellnik, I'm sure," Victoria exclaimed. "Where did he take you?"

"The last thing I remember is being in Archi Mac Dugan's office and talking to him. Then I woke up in an underground near New Eldorado City."

"It must be him," Victoria said again. "Didn't he tell you why and what he wanted from you?"

"He didn't have time," Bedford answered. "I was only locked up for a few hours. Then they were attacked by a very determined individual who probably put them on the run. During my escape—and I say this in all humility—I passed a group of people who were standing guard at the exit of the subway. I'm not sure if they were accomplices of this Buba Kellnik. But one thing is certain: as I passed them, I clearly heard the name Archi Mac Dugan. Still, I can't figure out what his involvement is."

"Your friend is definitely everywhere," Victoria said to John.

"Yes, you're right," John replied. "I think I've figured out what his role is in all of this. I'll tell you more when we find this Kellnik."

"Why have you arranged to meet me here?" asked Bedford.

"That's just it. We've been busy too. I regret to inform you that shuttle number three has sustained irreversible damage," John said in a disgruntled tone.

"What do you mean, irreversible?" Bedford asked, clearly worried.

"We'll discuss this later, if you don't mind."

Bedford didn't insist, but there was a look of concern in his eyes.

"For the time being, the reason I've asked you to meet me here is that, while we were investigating your kidnapper, our information led us to this address—which happens to be next door to where I used to live. Apparently, someone in these offices has been communicating with the network. My friend Jacky Collman has assured me that he can identify where these communications are coming from on the station, if we can determine where on Earth the source of their transmission originates."

"And is your friend Jacky sure where we'll find his men?" asked Bedford.

"Within 30 feet, yes," John replied.

"Let's go, gentlemen," Victoria concluded.

"Yes, but these offices have a very secure entrance. On the other hand, I haven't seen anyone go in or out since we got here. I find this unusually quiet for a Thursday morning. We'd have to go through my old building, which has a walkway connecting the two buildings at the level of the penthouse I used to occupy. I'm sure these offices are unoccupied and have some connection—other than physical—to my old apartment."

"I'm with you, John," Bedford said in an uncertain tone.

When they reached the top floor landing, John, Victoria and Gerald looked at each other, all three reluctant to go any further. The only weapon they had was a laser cutter that John had borrowed from his friend Jacky.

"I think we should ring the doorbell," Victoria said. "If someone answers, we'll just say we were invited down and look like idiots. At least we'll know who lives here."

Victoria pressed the doorbell in a frenzy. But nothing happened.

"There's no one there," Bedford remarked. "I guess we can go and come back later."

"No way," John said. "I'm here for answers, and a simple lock is not going to stop me."

John pulled out his laser cutter and set about forcing his way in. It took him only a few seconds to melt the lock pin. The next thing they knew, the three of them were inside the apartment. After taking a few steps towards the main room, they stopped dead in their tracks, all three surprised by what they saw.

"There's nothing here," Victoria exclaimed as she continued to explore the apartment. "It's completely empty—not a single piece of furniture, not even a chair."

"I don't get it," John said, shaking his head. "Jacky was sure the broadcasts from the station came here. There's got to be something hidden here or in the neighbouring offices."

"Maybe they've moved everything," Victoria said.

"No, they couldn't have," John replied. "They couldn't have known we were coming, and their last broadcast was less than 24 hours ago."

The three decided to search every nook and cranny of every room before heading out to the hallway leading to the offices. After several minutes of wandering around the apartment, Victoria and Bedford found John in what had been his bedroom. He stood motionless, scanning the far wall of the room.

"Something's wrong," Victoria said.

John didn't answer right away, too engrossed in his thoughts.

"Something is bothering me," John said. "I know that rooms vary in size according to their furnishings, but I have the strangest feeling that this room is longer or narrower than it was back then."

John moved to the back of the room and began tapping on various parts of the wall.

"Bingo," he exclaimed. "The wall sounds hollow. There must be something behind it. Come and help me."

The three of them searched the wall for an opening. John quickly saw that it was nothing more than a simple sheet of drywall that had been added during the apartment's renovation. Bedford pulled it aside to reveal the secret compartment behind it. John stuck his head through the opening. There was barely enough room for a man to stand. Then he looked down and saw an object the size of a shoebox. He took it out to examine it in the light of day.

"What is it?" asked Victoria.

"I have no idea," Bedford replied.

"It vaguely reminds me of something," said John. "It looks like a collector."

"A collector?" Victoria continued. "And can you tell me what it's for?"

"We used them during our army training to gather all kinds of information. These things are capable of collecting environmental data such as seismological, meteorological or even bacteriological readings. They can also act as relays, transmitting data wherever you want. This data was used by the military to determine the impact of bombs dropped on a target. But it's just a collector. It doesn't store all the data. It transmits most of it through the transmitter next to it."

"So we've got nothing," said a disillusioned Bedford.

"Not quite. I recognise the transmission frequency," replied John, who was operating the transmitter.

Bedford exclaimed in surprise.

"As head of security, it would be unforgivable if I didn't know," John continued. "It's a type of frequency we use on the station temporarily to create secure lines for short periods. It's often used during visits by heads of state.

"We now know that this is not where the terrorists communicated with the station, but where they gathered information and transmitted it to the station. Unfortunately, Jacky won't be able to tell us who on the station was receiving the information. It's a proprietary system whose data can only be read by a terminal using the same frequency. In the case of this collector, that type of terminal can only be found on Stargraber. The only way would be to have it analysed on the station to find out who the information was intended for. We'll also know what kind of information it was."

"I'd like to go," Bedford offered, relieved to finally be able to return to Stargraber.

"Very well," John replied. "In the meantime, Victoria and I will try to reach Buba Kellnik and get some answers."

"And how will you do that?" asked Bedford. "The last time I heard from him, he was running from muggers who shot at him. He could be anywhere by now."

"I don't think so," said John. "Even if Buba Kellnik did kidnap you, I think your escape was due to a moment of panic. From what you've told me, the shooting only lasted a few seconds. I don't think Buba Kellnik is a professional. I think he might have some interesting information to share with us that could shed some light on the situation. But I don't think he's behind any of this."

"But where do you think he might be?" asked Victoria.

"Strategically, I think he panicked, so he would have retreated to a place he knows well, where he feels protected."

"Do you think he went back to New Eldorado City?"

"Exactly. And that's where we're going," John concluded. "As for you, Bedford, focus all your efforts on deciphering the collector. The information you extract from this device may well be the key to understanding where this is all leading. As for us, we'll be in touch as soon as we have Buba."

John, Victoria and Gerald Bedford all left the apartment, determined to finally put a face to their real enemy.

Arriving in New Eldorado City, Victoria suggested that John stop by her mining concession before going in search of Buba Kellnik. There, they could rest for a while and pick up some weapons more effective than a laser cutter.

At the same time, Gerald Bedford arrived on Stargraber with his precious package. His first instinct was to lock himself in his office and pour himself a large glass of 12-year-old whisky to recover from his emotions. He quickly decided that he'd better find Archi Mac Dugan as soon as possible to have the collector's contents analysed. John and Victoria were counting on the results to put pressure on Buba Kellnik.

After pouring himself a second glass, he called his secretary.

"Berenice, have you found Mr Mac Dugan?"

"No, sir, and no one knows where he is," she replied, a little embarrassed not to be able to say more.

"Well, I suspected as much, so call me young Bronski—Desmond's assistant."

"Well, sir, would you like me to continue looking for Mr Desmond and Mr Mac Dugan?" she asked before leaving.

"No, I'll take care of it, Berenice. Thank you."

Gerald Bedford was at a loss. Not only did he not know why he had been kidnapped, but all the people directly under his command had a more or less close connection to the case. Not really knowing who to rely on, he thought it best to talk to someone he would never normally contact.

A few minutes later, Hubert Bronski entered Bedford's office.

"My little Hubert, I have a job for you," Bedford began.

"A mission, sir?" he said, amazed.

"Don't worry, nothing dangerous. Your father works on this station, doesn't he? If I'm not mistaken, he's in Mr Mac Dugan's research department."

"That's right, sir, but what does that have to do with me?" he asked curiously.

"I have a data collector here that I need analysed as soon as possible," Bedford replied. "Since Mr Mac Dugan is away, I can't entrust him with this task, but I'm sure your father has all the necessary expertise. I need the results of these analyses quickly, and I don't want to go through the usual channels."

"This is sensitive data, sir?" asked Bronski.

"Not really," replied Bedford, who didn't want to dwell on the problem. "It's more of a personal matter. That's why I need your help. I'm a little embarrassed to have the office do this analysis, so I'm relying on your discretion and that of your father. I want to know who the information was intended for, and what kind of information it was."

"You can count on me, sir," said Bronski, apparently only too happy to take on some responsibility. "If you like, I'll stay with my father until he's finished and report back to you as soon as possible."

"Yes, do that," Bedford replied. "I'd be grateful for the service."

Bedford took no chances. By calling John Desmond's young assistant, he knew the collector would arrive safely. The boy was too insignificant for anyone to suspect that he was in possession of one of the most important pieces of his investigation. On the other hand, analysis is usually done blind. Mathias Bronski, his father, would probably never know what he had analysed.

Meanwhile, back at the dealership, Victoria had had time to show John around. They spent some time studying the ramifications of the various galleries owned by Victoria and her competitors, trying to understand what the effects of the heatwaves from the station might be. John was amazed to see how extensive the tunnels were across several levels. The furthest reached the edge of Yellowstone Park. He wondered if one of Victoria's competitors might have been interested in eliminating their rivals, but nothing caught their attention. All the heatwaves were highly localised and, aside from endangering the lives of a few miners, their impact on the network as a whole was minimal.

After an hour, John and Victoria had no more answers. They had gone up to the well to see the damage caused by Victoria's diversion the day before, but it felt more like a Sunday walk than a real investigation. Both had let their minds wander on the way back to Victoria's compound. Still, they avoided revisiting the episode of Jacky's kiss. They were too preoccupied with the case that had them on the run—or so they claimed. With no hope of uncovering any more clues, they decided to set out again to flush out Buba Kellnik.

John, who had been waiting for the right moment to talk to Victoria but didn't know how, decided to stand in the doorway and speak his mind. As soon as he opened his lips, Victoria cut him off. She had sensed his repeated hesitation and knew he wanted to get something off his chest.

"I know exactly what you want to tell me," she said confidently.

For a moment, John recoiled, surprised by Victoria's aplomb.

"I... I... I was going to tell you to take something to cover yourself with. We may have to stand guard for a while, and I wouldn't want you to catch a cold."

"Of course..." Victoria replied mockingly. "It's very kind of you to think of that, but I'm perfectly capable of taking care of myself."

"As you wish," John replied. "But don't say I didn't warn you."

He turned and crossed the threshold, raising his eyebrows. He made his way as naturally as possible towards a Transplace coming their way. In the back of his mind, he seethed at having been so easily read. We've known each other less than 24 hours, and she already reads me like a book, he thought. How annoying! To calm himself, he told himself that he didn't even know what he wanted to say—so how could she?

As for Victoria, she was jubilant. Her little effect had hit the nail on the head. At the same time, she was glad he hadn't brought up the episode again. If, as she'd thought, he'd wanted to justify kissing her, she would've been in over her head. Do it well, talk about it much less. At the moment, her emotions were far too confused.

John and Victoria boarded the Transplace, which took them directly to the centre of New Eldorado City. They stopped two blocks from Buba Kellnik's office to plan a strategy for contacting him.

"Victoria, do you know if that jumble of stacked cubes they dare call an office has a back door?"

"Yes, of course," said Victoria. "If you go around the corner to the right, you'll find it."

"This is how it's going to work. According to you, there are three of them and only two of us. We need to divert their attention so I can surprise them. Since the simplest solutions are often the best, you're going to ring the doorbell. Buba will probably smell a trap. He'll want to make sure you're alone. Only then will he let you in— probably at gunpoint. My goal is to sneak into those offices in the short time between you ringing the bell and him wondering if it's a trap. Once inside, I'll just have to wait until you're in and his guard is down to surprise them."

Victoria, though not very reassured, felt comfortable with John. She left him to make his way down the alley and headed for Buba Kellnik's front door. Once across the square, she rang the bell as agreed. At first, there was no sound inside. Victoria waited a few moments and looked up at the security camera. This, she thought, would leave Buba in no doubt as to who had just rung the bell. Still nothing. The wait seemed interminable.

Had John had time to break into Kellnik's office?

Victoria started to ring the bell a second time, but just as her finger was about to touch the button, the door opened violently, and she found herself facing Buba with his gun pointed at her.

"Please, Victoria, come in, my darling," Buba said in a slightly haughty tone.

She complied and took one last look at the street behind her, as if she wasn't sure she would ever see it again.

"Buba, I don't know what you're doing with that gun, but I came here to talk business. It's the end of the month, if I'm not mistaken."

"Cut the crap, Victoria. I know exactly what you heard last night. I even saw you on board the station. Ever since I left this office, everything has gone wrong for me. I thought I was doing everything I could to stop it, but I've been short-circuited. I don't know who you told, but you're going to tell me nicely. I don't want to get into a fight with you."

He had barely finished his sentence when his two companions entered the room and nodded to him that they had found nothing.

"So you've come alone to throw yourself into the lion's den?" asked Buba rhetorically. "Well, that makes things easier, because I don't have much time for you."

Victoria noticed that he felt confident, sure that he was in control of the situation. Just then, John appeared behind Buba's two accomplices, and everything happened very quickly. He knocked out the one in front of him, and when the second one realised he was in danger, John was already behind him. He grabbed his wrist and twisted his arm, forcing him to the ground on one knee. John held him in that position, placing his knee between his shoulder blades and applying enough pressure to make his opponent flinch. At the same time, he made sure that Buba Kellnik's face was in the sights of his pistol.

Buba was stunned. With no time to react, he stood for long seconds, transfixed by the scene unfolding before his eyes, forgetting to aim the pistol at Victoria. Carried away by adrenaline, she reflexively punched Buba's hand to make him drop the gun.

Buba and his accomplices were now disarmed; John's plan had worked to perfection. He avoided showing that he was the first to be surprised. He knew he had put Victoria in great danger. Still, he was pleased to find that he had retained all his hard-won automatisms from his years of service.

"Don't move," John warned. "We need to talk. Victoria, pick up your gun and come to me. Point that gun at that man," he said, pointing at Buba Kellnik, "and if he moves, pull the trigger."

Victoria complied. Meanwhile, John took a quick look around for something to permanently restrain Buba's two accomplices. A coil of electrical wire lying on the floor was used to bind them securely.

"Great, now we can talk," John said in a perfectly controlled tone.

"I don't know you, and once I've told you what you want to know, what happens to us? I don't know what Victoria told you, but I don't trust you. Besides, I'm sure it was you who attacked us in the underground. You stopped me from getting the answers I wanted from this Mac Dugan, and now you've probably come to finish the job."

"Wait, I understand better now," John said, looking at Victoria. "You mean you kidnapped Archi Mac Dugan?"

"Yes, Victoria knows that, doesn't she, darling? I know you overheard us planning to kidnap her."

"Not at all," Victoria replied. "I thought you were going to attack the station."

John was beginning to make the connection between what had happened to him in the last few hours and the Buba Kellnik affair. Now, he had to clear up the grey areas.

"Why were you going to kidnap Mac Dugan?" asked John.

"I told you, I'm not going to tell you anything," Buba replied. "If you want to put a bullet in my head, go ahead."

"What if I told you that you didn't kidnap Archi Mac Dugan, but his boss—who is also my boss—the director of Little California on Stargraber, Mr Gerald Bedford?"

"Impossible," replied Buba. "We found him in his office, putting away his papers."

John reached into his wallet and pulled out an old newspaper article showing him with Jacky and Archi. The caption read that Archi Mac Dugan, Jacky Collman, and John Desmond broke the shooting record at the World Championships in Fresno.

"That's Mac Dugan on the right," John said, handing the article to Buba. "Do you recognise the man you kidnapped?"

Buba Kellnik was speechless as he realised he'd made a huge mistake. Victoria, equally embarrassed, listened to John's explanation, thinking she too had jumped to conclusions.

"I don't want to hurt you," John said. "I just want some answers. Victoria came to see me at ISS station yesterday because she thought someone was planning an attack. She thought it was you. After that, there were several attempts on our lives. When we did our research, we realised someone was watching you, so we wanted to meet you to find out why you were after Victoria and why you kidnapped Gerald Bedford. Archi Mac Dugan is my friend, and I can't believe he's behind all this."

Buba Kellnik was stunned by the newspaper article. How could he be so wrong?

"I don't know what to think anymore," Buba replied. "Yesterday, I thought I was doing the right thing. Today, I'm not so sure."

Victoria slowly approached Buba to express her support.

"We're not your enemies," she said. "I think everyone here wants to work together. Only by sharing information can we achieve our goal."

"I don't understand, I don't understand," Buba repeated, gesturing wildly. "We were convinced that we had Archi Mac Dugan. He's the one behind it all."

"Please continue," Victoria insisted.

Buba raised his head and straightened up, obviously ready to cooperate.

"We had a contact at the station. First, his associate came to see us here in New Eldorado City. He claimed to want to buy our underground mining concessions. It was obvious that this man knew nothing about mining in the field, but he had a very complete technical jargon. He returned several times. I think he was clumsily trying to gain our trust, because when we got carried away and told him firmly that we weren't interested in selling our galleries, his tone changed dramatically. It was at this point that he revealed the true nature of his visit. He told us he was a high-ranking security official from the American branch of Stargraber, and that he desperately needed our help. He made it clear that the station was under threat of attack, and that this was of direct concern to us, for if the station were destroyed, it was obvious that our selenium mines, which provide the raw material for the station's high-density solar panels, would lose over 80% of their value."

John and Victoria listened to Buba Kellnik's speech with great interest.

"His story sounded credible," Buba continued. "He told us the heatwaves coming from the station were tests aimed at collapsing the one-legged modules. Once the tests were complete, the terrorists would significantly increase the power to reach a critical temperature inside the one-leg modules, which would then implode, destroying the power transfer modules and, in a chain reaction, the entire station."

"Yes, but," John interrupted, "I'm sure a sudden power surge could only affect the entire station if every single one-legged module on Earth imploded simultaneously."

"That's what a scientist friend of ours told us," Buba agreed, surprised that John had such a precise opinion on the matter.

John and Victoria looked at each other in amazement. Buba Kellnik's version was very close to their own.

"We've already discussed this type of attack with one of John's colleagues," Victoria continued, "and we've come to the conclusion that it's not feasible. Every single person working on the station would have to be an accomplice for it to work."

"We came to the same conclusion," Buba Kellnik replied. "That's when I decided to question the person our contact had told us was responsible for the conspiracy—Archi Mac Dugan—by which I mean Gerald Bedford. My friends and I thought we'd get some answers and act accordingly. But that's when we were attacked in the galleries, and your friend escaped."

"Can you give me the name of your contact on Stargraber?" asked John.

"At this point, I don't see why not. The name of my contact on the station is John Desmond."

John met Victoria's eyes again, and she was almost more surprised than he was. He told himself that he was far from having cleared up all the grey areas.

"Your story is very interesting," John continued, "but it still contains one major flaw."

"I'll admit that we took the wrong person off the station," Buba continued, "but I can guarantee that my contact is reliable. Give me one good reason to doubt it."

"That's easy," John replied, pulling out his badge. "I'm John Desmond, Head of Security for Little California on Stargraber."

Buba Kellnik was so stunned that there was no reaction on his face. He pulled up a chair and sat down, adding:

"Victoria darling, there's a bottle of whisky in the bar. Bring it to me, you'll be fine."

Victoria brought him the bottle and a glass. In a flash, Buba put the glass down and drank straight from the neck.

"I feel utterly ridiculous," he added between sips. "I suppose it wasn't you who attacked us in the galleries?"

"No," John replied. "We were in New Albuquerque when it happened. This whole thing is driving me crazy. Every time we take one step forward, I feel like I'm taking two steps back. It's obvious the person we're looking for is very good at manipulating his world. Still, I'm sure—from his actions and the trouble he's going to—that there's a real conspiracy afoot."

"I agree," Victoria nodded. "At first, I thought he was after us, but now I think we're just inconvenient witnesses."

"I think you're right," John continued. "However, we do have a slight advantage over him. When our shuttle blew up, I think he thought we were dead. That's why we've been able to come and go as we please for the last 24 hours. But we've got to get back to the station to get to the bottom of this."

"I agree, John, but we don't know where to look or, more importantly, who to look for," Victoria said.

"How did you get in touch with him?" asked John, addressing Buba.

"He was the one who contacted us," Buba replied. "I'm sorry I can't help you. But I always thought he knew his business."

"We agree on that point," Victoria replied, "but unfortunately, knowing that he has good technical skills doesn't help us much."

"You don't understand," Buba said. "What I'm saying is that this man may be an excellent technician, but he's certainly not working as head of security. Besides, I've always thought he looked more like spaghetti than Louis XV furniture."

"So we need to find someone rather tall and wiry, working as a technician at the station. It can't be easy," said John. "We need more details. It's like looking for a needle in a haystack."

"Wait a minute, I'm remembering something," Buba added. "A couple of times, we took him to the elevators in the one-legged module. He always waited for us to leave before he went up. But only once did I see him go through the security gate reserved for station personnel. Someone was waiting for him on the other side. This person was younger than he was. If someone had asked my opinion at the time, I'd have bet it was his son. They seemed to know each other so well."

"So we're dealing with two people," John tried to summarise, "who know each other intimately, the leader of whom is an experienced technician, supposedly working on the American side of the station. He knows my name and rank, as well as the name and position of my best friend, Archi Mac Dugan. If he's as good a technician as you imply, then his level of accreditation must be quite high. This means two things. First, it should allow us to narrow our field of investigation without too much difficulty, and second, we're bound to know these traitors."

"It's a disturbing thought," Victoria added. "A man who may have smiled at you every day for months or years wants you dead! I think only by returning to the station can we find a way to stop him. Gerald Bedford will have gained valuable clues from the analysis of the collector we found."

"You're right, Victoria. We've got to get to Bedford, but we've got to give ourselves a little time to expose this impostor."

"Perhaps I can help you," said Buba. "When we kidnapped your friend Archi Mac Dugan... er, I mean Mr Bedford, we broke into the station using false health inspector identities. He opened every door for us, no questions asked. I think our cover is still good. Health inspectors are notoriously overzealous. A quick return like this will only strengthen your credibility."

"That's an excellent idea," said John. "I'd rather know you're here, but Victoria and I will return to the station with your identities to expose this traitor. If that man knows us, I'd rather he didn't know we were back at first. With any luck, he'll still think we crashed the shuttle. That will give us the time we need to work out a plan of action."

"It gives you a slight advantage. Let's hope it proves decisive," Buba pointed out.

"That's right, Mr Kellnik," John concluded. "We have to rely on ourselves and that slight advantage to neutralise him. I don't know who we're up against yet, but I hate him already."

Chapter Six
The Harder They Fall

John and Victoria arrived at Little California's elevator access control around 3 p.m. that afternoon. Victoria, who had never used this mode of transportation before, was amazed at the number of commuters and tourists in the elevators.

"Is it always this busy?" she asked.

"Yes, Victoria, and it's only early in the morning. That should make it easier for us to go unnoticed."

By the time she reached boarding control, Victoria felt her disguise growing heavier and heavier. She had to pass herself off as a thankless technician, and her lanky figure didn't help. Despite the cap hiding her long brown hair, she felt as if all eyes were on her. To ease her tension, she glanced around the oversized facility.

The boarding hall was identical to that of any airport: practical and soulless. The counters did not represent departing companies but the various accessible sections of the station. At this time of day, the most crowded desk was the visitors' desk. Many commuters were already there.

As John and Victoria made their way to the station's administrative check-in desk, Victoria's gaze fell further back on the elevator structure. Located about fifty yards from the concourse, the entrance to the elevators strangely resembled that of a futuristic theme park attraction. Long corridors decorated with photos and videos telling the history of the station ran uninterrupted.

The base of the installation must have been nearly a thousand feet in diameter and over 160 feet high. Higher up, all that remained was the giant tube climbing toward the clouds as far as the eye could see. At its centre were four elevators arranged like orange slices. Around the perimeter of the tube were cables transmitting energy harvested from the station. For purely aesthetic reasons, certain lower parts of the tube were translucent. The elevators, independent of each other, could be seen crossing one another.

The noise was also impressive. The elevators were driven by powerful electric motors, giving the impression of a giant toy at work. Most remarkable of all, however, was the ever-increasing speed. As soon as you reached the boarding hall, you could feel your stomach turning—a sensation identical to that experienced in the waiting area of a rollercoaster. This feeling became more pronounced as you approached the boarding gates. There, you could see the departing elevators of the station being catapulted into the sky.

The trip took only 15 minutes and covered almost 22,000 miles. The top speed of the elevators reached MACH 3, and the ride was supposed to be as smooth as taking the underground. To achieve this, only oversized electric motors with sufficiently gradual acceleration and deceleration capacity could support passengers without causing discomfort.

"Good morning, madam, monsieur," said a cybernetic hostess behind her counter. "May I see your tickets, please?"

"I'll never get used to these robots," said Victoria, still nervous.

"I hope our fake papers are above reproach," John said quietly in Victoria's ear. "If they're not, it'll be hard for me to charm them—despite their 90C."

Victoria smiled and nodded in agreement.

After passing through several checkpoints, they boarded one of the elevators.

"We can thank Buba. He's got a really good plan," Victoria said, relieved to have passed all the checkpoints. "I know we have nothing to blame ourselves for, but I feel guilty entering the station like this. This disguise as a health inspector makes me uncomfortable."

"Once we're aboard Stargraber, we can take it off. But for now, we can't let anyone know we're coming."

"What about Bedford? He expects us to call. I'm afraid he'll get impatient and send someone to get us."

"No, don't worry. He's probably busy enough at the station not to worry about us."

A voice came over the cabin loudspeakers.

"Ladies and gentlemen, Exppod is pleased to welcome you aboard this elevator to Stargraber. Your transfer is estimated to take 18 minutes. Please ensure your seat belts are securely fastened. Departure is imminent, so please prepare to recline your seats."

At that moment, each seat reclined 45° in preparation for take-off. A moment later, an irresistible thrust was felt. Victoria loved the sensation as it gently pushed her back into the seat. After a minute or so, they automatically straightened to allow the occupants to move around the cabin.

John figured this was the perfect time to finally find out if his charm had worked on Victoria. He straightened in his seat. After ordering a snack, he turned back to her and tried to meet her gaze to assert his presence.

"You still haven't told me what you think of that kiss at Jacky's," she said with a broad smile, turning to face him.

John was taken aback by Victoria's aplomb. This was the second time she'd surprised him. He didn't even know how to answer the question. He'd racked his brain for hours, trying to avoid appearing boorish—and now, in the blink of an eye, he was wondering how not to appear too shy.

Victoria smiled mischievously, seeing the turmoil in John's mind and not quite knowing how to react. Her feminine intuition had not failed her. John, often self-assured, tended to tense up when he had to confront his feelings. His micro-reactions confirmed it.

She had a hunch their affair would last longer than the investigation. John was obviously looking for an elegant way to answer, but he couldn't take his eyes off Victoria's green eyes.

To shorten his agony, Victoria decided to take the lead again.

"All right," she said. "Since you won't answer me, I'll just have to find out for myself."

As she said these words, Victoria moved closer to John and kissed him again—this time with more conviction. John was glad he didn't have to answer her. The other travellers watched with amusement and envy. John and Victoria were undeniably reminiscent of a young couple in love.

"I wonder how you've managed to beat me again," John said, coming to his senses.

Victoria couldn't suppress an open smile, very pleased with her small effect. For the rest of the ride, they chatted as if they were fifteen years old, giving each other a well-deserved break.

As they approached the terminus, they both resumed their respective roles as health inspectors, on the lookout for the slightest infraction.

As soon as they disembarked, John, who knew the station inside and out, quickly distinguished himself from the stream of passengers.

"We'll use the corridors again," he told Victoria. "I'm pretty well known around here and I don't want to be recognised before I've seen Bedford. It'll take longer than using the Navigon, but we have to be discreet."

After traversing the station's darkest corridors, John and Victoria finally arrived at the administrative offices. John passed through his own office and went directly to Bedford's without being seen. As head of security, John had direct access to the Director's office through a back door.

Gerald Bedford was sitting behind his desk, initialling the morning's many files as usual. John and Victoria entered the back door at the same time.

John, Victoria, I'm glad to see you, Gerald Bedford said, hardly surprised to see them.

Were you expecting us? asked Victoria, again a little surprised by Bedford's lack of reaction.

Not at all, he replied, and if I may add, I find your attire very appropriate.

And can we find out why? asked John.

Given the situation, I think the only thing left to do is to search the station from top to bottom. In that case, your health inspector outfits will come in very handy.

What situation? asked Victoria.

I've been trying to reach you all morning without success. Not knowing what had happened to you, I assumed you wanted to remain invisible. If the situation seems so desperate, it's because I have the analysis results from the collector. When I arrived at the station, my first move was to ask your friend Archi for help, but he was nowhere to be found. No one has seen him since you left. I didn't press the matter at the time, thinking I was in the best of hands.

So I asked your assistant, young Bronski, to have his father analyse the collector. It seemed the right thing to do. Mathias Bronski is an experienced analyst. He's been working here for a long time, never asks any questions, and retrieving data from a collector is as natural to him as going to the coffee machine.

What bothers me is that young Bronski has brought me the results, and they are negative. And when I say negative, I mean we don't have any results. For fear of arousing suspicion, I didn't want to ask for a second verification analysis. The only thing left to do was to find Archi Mac Dugan. Only he could have done a second analysis without attracting further suspicion. Unfortunately, without moving heaven and earth, my search was in vain. Which is why I'm so glad you've finally arrived. Together, we'll have a much better chance of finding your friend.

To sum up the situation, John said, we have nothing, and even less than yesterday. I think you're right, Gerald, we need to find Archi and do a second analysis. Then we'll decide.

Gerald, you could use your status to make a surprise inspection of the services, which would give you access to many parts of the station without raising too many questions. As for us, we'll continue to act as health inspectors and look for Archi in the less glamorous parts of the station. Since I'm sure we're being watched, we won't use the usual means of communication. We'll meet back here in an hour.

Very good, John, Bedford continued. We'll say here in 60 minutes.

Gerald Bedford left on his own, and John, accompanied by Victoria, also set off in search of Archi.

Our only hope, John told Victoria, is that our invisible enemy has finally made his first mistake. If we're lucky and he's panicked, he's probably kidnapped Archi to find out if we've already exposed him. That's why Bedford hasn't been able to track him down.

And that's good news? asked Victoria, in a slightly sarcastic tone.

Yes, I think so, because the kidnapper must need Archi's skills to complete his project. He doesn't have much time, and he knows we're on to him. He must be holding Archi somewhere on the station. I know every inch of that damned space submarine. I guarantee we'll find him in less than an hour.

For his part, Gerald Bedford searched every visible part of the station. He went from cabin to apartment, from refectory to closet, from corridor to staircase, from opening to opening… without the slightest result.

As for John and Victoria, spending so much time in the most unkempt areas of the station was quickly wearing down their outfits.

I'm seriously running out of ideas, John said to Victoria, and we've only got 20 minutes before we're back with Bedford.

I'm willing to assist you, she replied, but my knowledge of the station is limited, so I don't see how I can help you other than morally. I'd have to be the one who built this thing to know more about it than you do.

You're great, Victoria, John said, his eyes suddenly brightening.

Victoria pretended to roll her shoulders, not really knowing why she was so great.

Awesome, I tell you, awesome, he repeated. When the station was built, pressurised working airlocks were installed at the ends of each module. These were no more than two dozen square feet in size and made it possible to control module assembly without having to pressurise the whole thing. This saved considerable time in the construction and assembly of the station.

Subsequently, these tiny parts were abandoned. Since they were independent of the modules, and given their small size, it would have been more complicated to reintegrate them than to forget them. In short, these airlocks were perfect hiding places.

And you think someone could have hidden Archi in there? asked Victoria.

I think it's the only place we haven't checked, John replied. If the people we're looking for know the station well, then it's the best place for them to keep someone prisoner—completely invisible to everyone—while still being able to interrogate them at will.

John decided to take a Navigon to get to the end of the section he was in as quickly as possible. He figured that even if someone recognised him, he didn't have much to lose. This was their last chance to find Archi.

The Little California assembly airlock was just behind the shuttle docking platform. Once there, John led Victoria through a service door into a storage room for shuttle spare parts. The room was a disorganised mess. Numerous crates were scattered here and there, and only two shelves on opposite walls held the smallest samples.

This is it, John said, turning on his heel to examine the room. Help me look, Victoria. Behind one of these crates, we should find a trapdoor that will lead us to that famous airlock.

I'll take the left side, Victoria said.

After a few minutes, Victoria moved a crate that seemed lighter than the others. Very dusty, it looked as if it had been placed there for decoration.

I think I've got something, Victoria exclaimed.

Yes, that's right, John said, brushing the dust off a handle built into the partition with his hand. Look, Victoria, there are clear signs that this handle has been used recently. We're not the first people to use this passageway since it was closed. I have a feeling we're on the right track.

With a flick of his wrist, John unlocked the narrow entrance they had to crawl through.

Do you want me to go this way? asked Victoria.

No, I'd rather you wait for me here. If anyone comes, put the crate back in front of the hatch and hide. I won't be long.

John clenched his flashlight between his teeth and began to make his way through what looked more like an air shaft than an access corridor. The station's designers had kept this passageway narrow in the unlikely event that they ever needed to use these airlocks again.

After a few feet, John came to a very narrow space where the only door leading to the airlock was located. Turning the handle to open the heavy metal door, he prayed he would not find nothing but emptiness. The door opened slowly with a creak that seemed to echo to the edge of the room. Mechanically, John looked around, as if to make sure he wasn't being followed, before entering the room.

No sooner had he stepped into the enclosed space than he heard a muffled moan from his right. He turned his flashlight in that direction and saw his friend lying on the floor, tied up like a sausage.

"I'm here, Archi," John said reassuringly, as he began to untie him.

It took Archi Mac Dugan a while to realise it was indeed his friend leaning over him. His throat was so dry, he felt as if an entire hourglass had been poured down it.

"A pool, I need a pool," Archi stammered.

"Do you think you can swim at a time like this?" said John. "You never cease to amaze me, my friend."

"Not at all," Archi replied painfully, "but I'm so thirsty I could drink a whole swimming pool."

The two men laughed for a moment before John took Archi by the arm and led him towards the exit.

Victoria waited anxiously for John's return. Time seemed to pass more slowly than usual. After about ten minutes, she finally saw the flickering beam of light that announced John's return. She had expected him to appear at any moment, alone and defeated. How likely was it that Archi would be in the airlock?

In an instant, following that thought, she saw Archi Mac Dugan's head emerge from the tiny hatch. For a moment, Victoria thought she was witnessing a second birth, so much did Archi struggle to pull himself out, grunting. She hastened to help him out of his prison and let out a huge sigh of relief. Once John had followed his friend, they congratulated each other for a few long seconds before deciding to head back to Gerald Bedford's office.

In the Navigon that took them back to Bedford's office, Archi had time to regain his composure and began to tell the story of his abduction. Unfortunately, there was nothing in his account to indicate who had done it.

Back in the administrative quarters, Gerald Bedford waited for John and Victoria to return, as agreed. Their arrival in Archi's company reassured him.

"Archi, I'm glad to see you, but where the hell have you been?" asked Bedford.

"I've been kidnapped," Archi replied calmly.

"Kidnapped?" he asked in surprise. "From the station? But for what?"

"We don't know," John continued. "Archi gave us a detailed account of his abduction, but unfortunately, he never got to see the faces of his captors."

"Maybe you've heard something that can help us?" asked Victoria.

"I'm sorry, but I don't remember anything specific, although I did hear them talking. In fact, I think there were only two of them, but none of their conversations caught my attention," Archi said, obviously annoyed at not being able to provide more details.

"Don't think about it," Bedford said. "You're here safe and sound; that's all that matters. Besides, you're going to be able to help us. I need you for a little expertise. Your friend John picked up a data collector on Earth that was connected to one of the station's beams. We need to know what's in it. The data in the flash memory could lead us to the people we're looking for."

"I'd be happy to," Archi replied. "A little work will allow me to relieve some of the stress of my abduction."

"Especially since you seem to be the only one really competent in this field," said John.

"Oh, really?" exclaimed Archi, touched by the compliment.

"We're running around in circles here," Victoria added. "We need a lead, and we thought the data contained in this collector would lead us to the instigator of the whole thing."

"Yes," Bedford continued. "And I've already tried to get Bronski to analyse it, but to no avail. He told me there was no useful data."

"Bronski is a very capable man," said Archi, reaching for the collector Bedford was holding.

"Yes, but apparently, he doesn't have your talent," John added, hoping to motivate him.

Archi didn't look up, already absorbed in examining the collector. As he watched, something seemed to be bothering him. He kept turning the object over and over, but his mind was elsewhere.

"Is everything all right?" Victoria asked, noticing his discomfort.

"Mmh, mmh," he mumbled.

Suddenly, he exclaimed, "That's it, I know," as he continued to work with the collector.

"What do you know? What's in it? Well, kudos to you if that's what it is. I'll never doubt you again," John said, turning to the others with a cheerful expression.

"Not at all; there's nothing in there, not a single piece of data. I'm sure of it."

"I'm lost," said Victoria, raising her eyes to the sky as if praying to the divine.

"No better," added Bedford in dismay. "Will you tell us what you're talking about?"

"You won't find any data in this collector because it was erased by the assailant, kidnapper or terrorist—call them what you will."

"You mean we brought back an empty collector?" asked John.

"Not at all," Archi answered. "The memory of the station has been erased by the person we're looking for."

John and Victoria turned mechanically to Bedford, who had been holding the object long enough.

"Don't look at me like that," he insisted. "I had nothing to do with this."

"I was thinking of Bronski," Archi continued. "When Victoria asked me to remember if I'd heard anything, it didn't occur to me at the time. But when Gerald handed me the collector and told me he'd had it analysed by Bronski, I made the connection.

"When I was locked in the airlock, I was blindfolded, but I could see my feet. At one point, my captor dropped an object. I didn't see his face when he picked it up, but I'm sure it was the collector. I didn't pay much attention at the time, but on closer inspection, I bet it was that very collector I saw fall into my dungeon."

"I agree with you," said John. "Remember," he added, turning to Victoria, "back on Earth, your friend Buba Kellnik told us he saw his mysterious interlocutor meet a man in the station's elevator lobby who he could have sworn was his son, so close did they seem."

"You're absolutely right, John," Victoria added. "In fact, he told us he thought he looked more like a technician than a head of security, referring to his puny appearance—and that fits Bronski Sr.'s physique."

"Bronski? That can't be him!" Bedford said, looking defeated. "I've given our enemy the only evidence we had. I'm unforgivable."

"It's not your fault," Victoria tried to reassure him. "How could you have known?"

"It doesn't matter," said John. "We know who we're dealing with now, and they don't know we know their identities. We have to take advantage of that. The sooner we get our hands on them, the harder they'll fall."

Chapter Seven

A Huge Gulp Of Air

To save time, Bedford, like a good tactician, had divided up the tasks. For him, catching these traitors was like a game of chess, at which he was accustomed to excel. His task was simple: he had to seal off the station to cut off the Bronskis' retreat, while sending his troops to attack the enemy positions. In theory, everything seemed easy. In practice, he had sent Archi and Victoria to the elevators to prevent any retreat in case one of them slipped through the net, while John had gone with some guards to the technical labs to arrest Mathias Bronski.

Hubert Bronski paced nervously through the narrow corridors of the station. His father had entrusted him with a task of the utmost importance, and he didn't want to disappoint him. He had to get Mac Dugan's personal access codes, find out what he knew, and get rid of him. Eliminating Archi Mac Dugan would be no problem. One well-placed blow, and it would be over. Lying to cover up his crime was second nature to him. What made him nervous was getting a confession. He'd have to hold an innocent man's gaze and probably torture him to get what he wanted. Hubert Bronski was a coward, more used to underhanded tactics than direct confrontation.

As he approached the spare parts store leading to the airlock, his heart began to race. Success would inevitably earn him his father's approval, and perhaps a place of choice in the new world order he wanted to create.

First things first, he told himself. First discover what Mac Dugan knew, then fame.

Hubert Bronski moved the crate in front of the hatch to the airlock, opened it, and slipped into the narrow tunnel. He opened the door leading to the tiny room where Mac Dugan had been held and stepped inside.

Hubert remained frozen for several seconds before letting out a cry of rage. Mac Dugan had obviously escaped, or someone had helped him. Either way, his failure would not go without consequence. Mechanically, he turned around to make sure the square metre of space was empty. Examining the ropes left on the floor, Hubert realised that Mac Dugan had been helped to escape. The knots he had carefully tied had simply been untied.

He didn't know what to do and circled the room like a caged lion. He knew he had to tell his father, but doing so would be an admission of failure. Not telling him would be an unforgivable mistake. He had to make a choice: call his father and face his wrath, or find Mac Dugan himself and finish the job.

John arrived near the technical labs, accompanied by two guards, to arrest Mathias Bronski. He wondered what kind of man he would find before him. Obviously, Bronski had succeeded in deceiving the world by hiding his true nature. John was aware that he had only a slight advantage. Bronski didn't know that he had been identified, but he did know that John was looking for the person who had tried to kill him.

His plan was simple: engage in a banal conversation under the pretext of a security problem, while involving the guards. He would wait for the right moment to arrest Bronski without hurting anyone. He knew that even with the guards, Bronski wouldn't act until he was sure he had been exposed.

"Gentlemen, here's the plan," he told the guards, explaining the operation in detail. "To prepare the ground, I'll enter alone. You will follow exactly two minutes later, giving me time to let you into the room. Once inside, you'll pretend to search thoroughly in the places I'll indicate. We've already had security alerts, and I think that after a few minutes, he won't pay any attention to your movements.

"While you continue your investigation, slowly approach us. When I give you the signal, we'll move into action. We must be quick and efficient. Since I'm closest to Bronski, I'll restrain him and you come in to cuff him. If all goes well, he won't be hurt, and it'll all be over in no time."

Mathias Bronski's laboratory was one of the largest and most atypical of all. The Hydroponics Research Laboratory was used to improve our knowledge of growing food in different environments. It was the only room to benefit from a glass dome. The lab staff had requested this feature so that the cultures could have direct access to sunlight.

This particular dome had received the utmost attention during construction. In constant contact with the sun's direct rays during the day, it was equipped with self-adapting synthetic glass panels that mimicked Earth-like exposure conditions. At night, the panels became completely transparent, providing a unique view of the Milky Way. It was as if one were being projected into the heart of the stars.

"Gentlemen," said John, glancing at his watch, "it's 7.30. Two minutes to go. Good luck."

John entered the double airlock. Bronski, bent over his work, looked up as he heard the unmistakable sound of decompression from the first airlock door. In an effort to appear as natural as possible, John gave him a friendly wave through the thick glass partition that still separated him from the laboratory. Bronski responded mechanically without paying further attention. John was relieved to see that Bronski suspected nothing and lowered his head to avoid revealing his satisfaction.

After passing through the second airlock door, John naturally went to the pressure suits to put on one of his own. He hated sweating in the outfit, but protocol required that everyone entering the lab be equipped with one. This was to prevent the risk of contaminating the cultures with external germs. Since the colour-coded contamination risk indicator above the final access door was minimal, the pressurised helmet was not mandatory. John thought this would make his job easier. If the suit had been fully pressurised, his and the guards' movements would have been severely restricted.

Another advantage, he thought. This arrest was definitely going well.

John finally entered the lab. The nearly 1,000 square metres in front of him looked more like 2,000. The multitude of small greenhouses, culture tanks—some four to six storeys high—irrigation pipes running in all directions, UV lamps, and mirrors to maximise the light, along with the majestic dome over 50 feet high, created an overwhelming sense of scale.

John's eyes were drawn to two man-sized greenhouses on either side of the room, each with its own secondary airlock. These were used to create specific atmospheric environments independent of the rest of the lab. He began to think he had done the right thing by bringing his men with him. Alone, it would have been difficult to control every exit.

John approached Bronski with a detached air, preparing for his men's intervention. Bronski was fully occupied with his activities and didn't immediately raise his head. For a brief moment, John felt he could have overpowered him alone, but he didn't want to take any chances and stuck to the plan. Bronski, having successfully concealed his identity, might well be armed or a martial arts expert.

Bronski stood in the middle of the lab, bent over a small growing tray, presumably for taking cuttings. On the surrounding work surface were his helmet, tweezers, several pots of seedlings, and several charts for recording various experiments.

"Good morning, Mr Bronski," said John, beginning the discussion. "How are you, Mr Bronski?"

"Fine, thank you. To what do I owe the honour of a visit from the Head of Security?"

"Just an inspection," said John. "I can see you're busy, and I don't want to bother you too long. Some of my men will be joining us to inspect the lab. We just want to make sure everything is in order here. We've received several messages recently that lead us to believe an organisation may be planning to steal information about our research. We want to ensure they haven't planted bugs in the labs."

John was careful to be as vague as possible about the threats he referred to in order to appear more credible.

"I understand, Mr Desmond, but please hurry; I've got a lot of work to do," Bronski said calmly.

From the way he answered, John knew immediately that his plan was going to work. Bronski, too absorbed in his work, was unaware of what lay ahead.

"There they are," John replied, pointing to the entrance hatch, "and it won't take more than a few minutes."

John waved his men through the glass surfaces of the airlock and invited them to enter. Once inside, he spread them out to the four corners of the room, instructing them to look for any signs of sabotage.

So as not to arouse suspicion, each of his deputies set about exploring every nook and cranny. Given the size of the room, John estimated it would take several minutes for his men to reach him and be ready to arrest Bronski without drawing attention. So, John began the conversation as naturally as possible to keep engaged with his target.

A few moments later, Mathias Bronski raised a finger to interrupt the conversation and turned away, assuming the characteristic position of someone receiving a call on their Gcom and wishing to keep the conversation private.

Hubert Bronski was struggling. His hand was shaking, and he could barely hold the glass he'd picked up at the bar of the Lunar One restaurant. His father was on the line, and now he had to tell him that Archi Mac Dugan wasn't dead—worse, he'd escaped and was nowhere to be found.

"Hello, Father, I don't have very good news..."

At the other end of the line, Mathias Bronski nodded in agreement as he strode into the room.

Each of John's men turned mechanically to meet his gaze. No doubt they thought this call was the right time to intervene. John gave them a discreet signal to wait. He didn't want to deviate from the original plan. Also, taking advantage of the delay, John decided to contact Victoria and Archi to let them know Hubert Bronski was not with his father. He slowly walked away from Mathias.

"Victoria, it's John. How are you getting on with the elevators?"

"We're not far off," she replied. "Everything is fine here. We're on our way to the mechanical rooms. But we've only just arrived at Lunar One. Archi tells me that he deserves a beer."

"All right, go ahead. For my part, I'll finish the little inspection we talked about, but there's one essential element missing. I'll join you to finish lunch."

John tried to be as evasive as possible so as not to arouse Mathias Bronski's suspicions and to make Victoria understand that Bronski's capture was only a matter of minutes away.

"Just a second," said Victoria.

A silence followed.

"I can't believe it, we've just spotted young Bronski," Victoria continued. "Just my luck! He's right in front of us at the restaurant bar. I think we'll finish our inspection before yours—and with a bonus," she added, in a slightly sarcastic tone.

"Very well," John replied as casually as possible. "Anything else?"

John's and Mathias Bronski's eyes met from time to time, and both exchanged occasional light chuckles as they watched each other's conversation.

"I can't tell you anything in particular," Victoria said, "except that he's talking to his Gcom right now. That should make it easier for us to catch him—he won't see it coming."

John decided to end the conversation. A shiver ran down his spine. Maybe Mathias Bronski was talking to his son at the same time. If so, he had to act quickly before he was caught off guard.

"Thank you for all the information. I'll see you at lunch as agreed—don't order without me. I'll be right back."

John hung up without another word, and Victoria looked at Archi with a shrug.

"Not happy, little John," she said. "I don't think he likes the fact that we're going to arrest our Bronski before his. He practically hung up on me, telling me to wait for him to arrest our young Bronski, I think."

"I rather think he couldn't speak freely," Archi pointed out. "He probably wanted you to understand that trying to arrest him in such a crowded place could be risky. We'll follow him when he's finished and stop him in a more suitable place. There's no need to wait, John—between the two of us, we'll soon get the better of this young pipsqueak."

For his part, John had only let his hesitation show for a split second. He understood that the Bronskis were talking and that young Hubert, if he hadn't already done so, would soon reveal to his father that Archi was free. Mathias Bronski would then realise that Archi would certainly have told his friend the name of his kidnapper. He would then realise that John wasn't there for a simple inspection, but to arrest him.

John had only seconds to stop Bronski before it was too late. He looked around for his two colleagues to give them the signal.

John didn't immediately realise that while talking to his son, Bronski had made his way to one of the lab's two pressurised greenhouses, connected by an airlock. Realising that Bronski was so close to an exit, John gave the signal to intervene—but it was too late. He moved towards Mathias Bronski and, watching his arm, couldn't help but utter a frightened cry.

"No!" cried John. "Mathias, don't do this. You're crazy!"

Bronski was holding a laser pruning shear. Very useful in a hydroponic greenhouse, this device could also prove extremely dangerous if misused. Extremely versatile, it could be used to prune a bonsai tree or to cut branches several dozen inches long.

Mathias Bronski, well aware of the device's capabilities, had turned it into a handgun by slamming it into the corner of a piece of furniture to expose the laser lens. He now aimed it at the laboratory dome. A powerful discharge from the shears sent Bronski reeling.

The entire dome shook from the impact, but did not give way. John's two colleagues rushed to Bronski's side, trying to stop him before he had time to fire the shears again.

From his military experience, John knew that his colleagues would never have time to cover the distance to Bronski before he fired again. So, he looked for an alternative. It seemed to him that the main airlock was out of reach. Neither of the two pressurised greenhouses could be reached in the time available. If the dome were to give way, he would first have to be able to breathe and withstand the decompression.

Keeping an eye on Bronski, John grabbed a nearby helmet and locked it onto his suit. At the same moment, a second explosion sounded. The dome continued to resist, but cracks began to appear in the synthetic glass panels that made up the structure. The balance of the entire structure was compromised.

Bronski knew that the next blast would cause the dome to implode under the pressure. He entered one of the pressurised greenhouses. All he had to do was fire one last shot before sealing the greenhouse entrance with the remaining power of his shears and disappearing. Seeing John's men closing in fast, Bronski, aware of the implications of his gesture, had no hesitation.

Violent cracks were heard. John knew the dome was about to give way. He had only a few seconds to tie himself down wherever he could to withstand the shock of decompression and avoid being sucked into space. John grabbed a strap lying on one of the workbenches and wrapped his arm around a pole that seemed to be sealed to the floor. As for his men, they had chosen another option and were trying to reach the nearest exit. One of them had managed to reach the greenhouse through which Bronski had fled and was desperately trying to open the pressurised door that Bronski had jammed in his escape.

For a moment, John realised that one of his colleagues had made the right choice, as he was less than a metre from the exit. He was already reaching out to press the airlock switch. John looked down at his arm to make sure it was properly strapped.

Suddenly, a deafening noise filled the room. John looked up. The dome had collapsed. A shrill hiss followed almost immediately. The air was already being sucked into the sidereal void. John's colleagues stopped dead on their way out. For a brief moment, they were frozen, as if suspended in mid-air, completely motionless. The next moment was terrifying. They were being violently pulled towards the hole that had formed in the dome.

The air had already become so thin that even the screams of the last of his men, clinging to the small handle of the airlock with all his might, soon became inaudible. It was only a matter of seconds before the lack of oxygen and the pressure forced him to let go, throwing him back into the icy space.

John was in bad shape. The force of the impact had nearly torn his arm off, and only the hastily attached strap prevented him from knowing the fate of his colleagues. Fortunately, the pressure suit had withstood the shock, and he could breathe. Now, the strap would have to hold for another few dozen seconds until all the air had been expelled.

John stared at the strap as if to tell it not to move, but the more he looked at it, the more it slipped inexorably. In a moment, he too would be catapulted into space. As the seconds ticked by, his gaze became more intense: "Don't slip, don't slip," he urged himself. John began to feel the pull weakening. There was hardly any air left under the dome. Just a few more seconds, he thought.

The harness was now held together by just a few fibres, and the pressure was dropping in unison. John was beginning to think he was safe when suddenly the harness gave way. The force of the ejection had diminished considerably, but John was still moving inexorably towards the gaping hole at the speed of a grandmother in a walker.

In his misfortune, John considered himself lucky. Since his speed wasn't that great, he still had a chance to grab onto the rest of the structure before he was lost in space.

Just a few more feet and he'd know his fate. Unable to influence his trajectory, John resolved to remain calm in order to conserve his oxygen. A multitude of thoughts ran through his mind. He suddenly realised that he hadn't touched a glass of alcohol since he'd met Victoria and they'd been drawn into this affair—nor had he felt the need to; except at this very moment.

The thought made him smile, but the proximity of the dome structure brought him back to his senses. The two-by-two-metre opening came closer and closer.

Observing the gaping hole, John decided to cross himself, as women are wont to do in the marital bed, to occupy as much space as possible and maximise his chances of clinging to the dome. According to his calculations, at least one of his limbs should touch the remaining structure. He'd watched his wife occupy almost the entire four square metres of their king-size bed, so he was sure, at 5'8", that he would hit an intact part of the dome. He just prayed it was one of his hands.

As he made contact, John felt a slight pressure on the back of his hand. He twisted his wrist and managed to grab it with his fingertips. Now, all he had to do was stabilise himself.

John breathed a sigh of relief under his helmet and secured his grip with his other hand. He was almost saved. His feet floated in the vastness of space, but his hands held him firmly to the station's dome. He looked around, stunned by the cold beauty of the space around him. For a few long seconds, he was blinded by the multitude of stars he felt he could touch with his fingertips.

Knowing his air supply was limited, John looked back towards the dome, thinking he could pull on his arms to propel himself back into the station. But then he realised there was no going back. In fact, by the time he had manoeuvred to hold on, a great deal of debris had accumulated at the top of the dome, almost completely blocking the opening through which he had been nearly thrown to his certain death.

John tried in vain to push the debris inward. Unfortunately, he could only use one arm and had no support. The residual pressure, no doubt maintained by an air leak from one of the claws, was still enough to keep the debris at the top of the structure and prevent it from falling back down.

He needed to find another way out.

He glanced at his air gauge. Fifteen minutes. Enough time to find a way out, he thought. Glancing around, Stargraber's outer hull seemed particularly flat. A feeling of panic came over him.

"Think, John, think," he repeated to himself.

Continuing his self-motivation, he tried again to push down the debris blocking the passage. After several attempts, he felt it move. The damaged greenhouse seemed to have emptied itself of air. This allowed the pressure to drop enough to finally push the debris back into the dome.

He looked at his air gauge again: six minutes. Time was passing much faster than he had estimated. He checked it again, thinking he'd misread it: five minutes. He redoubled his efforts, waving frantically. The debris collided, dropping slightly but systematically rising again, still blocking access to the only passage.

Four minutes.

The only solution he could think of was to force his way through. If he moved fast enough, John would be able to get through the debris even if he couldn't push it back. There was no time to wait for them to come down on their own.

Like a spelunker, John set out to find his way in headfirst. His only concern was his suit. Would it be strong enough? It wasn't designed for this kind of sport. One look at his wrist convinced him: two minutes. His suit had held up so far, and his air supply couldn't wait any longer.

After a few more efforts to free himself from the pile of objects jammed together in the rift, John found himself back on the right side of the structure, inside the station. He felt as if he'd been reborn.

But before he could breathe the good old recycled air of the station again, he had one last exercise to do. He had to reach the main airlock fifty feet below. He positioned himself upside down and leaned on the debris to propel himself towards the exit. He had to measure his effort precisely to reach the airlock, but not give too strong an impulse that would cause him to bounce.

He looked again at his gauge, which had begun to flash, telling him he had less than a minute. He had only one try.

Estimating the strength he needed, John held his breath and propelled himself by instinct. The descent seemed only slightly faster than the ascent as the air in his suit began to thin.

He had reached his destination, and with one last effort, he grabbed the airlock handle, pushed the opening button, and the airlock closed behind him. He was now in the airlock, the door sealed, and the unmistakable sound of pressurisation was heard. The room filled with air. John fell to his knees, tore off his helmet and swallowed a huge gulp of air.

Chapter Eight
For A Surprise!

Victoria and Archi had decided to follow John's advice and not intervene in the restaurant. Archi knew from experience that young Bronski was tough and that they would have to take him by surprise to stop him smoothly.

They both followed him out of the restaurant, waiting for the right moment to grab him.

"We've been following him for almost five minutes, you know. When are you going to stop him?" asked Victoria.

"I have no idea," Archi replied. "I never realised that this station could hold so many people. We can't put these people in danger; we have to wait until there's no one around. If this continues, we'll stop him over China."

"All right," Victoria said. "I'll take it from here."

"Do you have a plan, my dear, if I may pry?"

"It's very simple," Victoria replied, lifting her chin, obviously proud of her idea. "I'm going to use you as bait."

Archi's Adam's apple made a characteristic to-and-fro movement, and his eyebrows raised in perfect synchronicity.

"I think this is a very bad idea. I'd even go so far as to say it's a lousy plan," Archi protested. "Let me remind you that this would-be psychopath almost killed me the first time. If he targets me, I can only count on you to get me out of his clutches."

"Thanks for the vote of confidence," Victoria said dryly.

"Don't get me wrong, I have full confidence in you," Archi was quick to add. "But have you seen the size of this beast? I heard that when he was born, the midwife thought his mother was expecting triplets."

"Don't worry, Archi. Don't forget that I've worked in mines all my life, and I've been confronted with large, panic-stricken co-stars in narrow tunnels on more than one occasion. I know how to deal with them."

As she finished her sentence, Victoria grabbed Archi's arm and placed three of her fingers strategically on his wrist. A second later, Archi was on his knees.

"I understand," Archi said, rising to his feet. "Remind me to ask you for a new arm for Christmas," he added, massaging his shoulder. "Our young friend seems to know where he's going, though. He hasn't hesitated since we started following him. I can tell you that even I, after all these years, sometimes hesitate at certain forks in the road. My guess is that we're heading for the Lightstocks mobile warehouse."

"And what is that?" asked Victoria.

"The place where we store anything smaller than a cubic metre," Archi answered. "It's like the basement of the station. Anyone can put whatever they want there. I generally avoid going there, as it's an impenetrable labyrinth to the uninitiated."

"It's perfect," said Victoria. "Since you've already been there, we have a slight advantage over him. We'll catch him there."

"We may have the advantage, but it won't be a walk in the park. Mobile warehouses are aptly named. Each container, called a 'cubic', consists of nine cubes of one cubic metre each on three levels, sort of like a giant Rubik's cube. They can be moved as needed. It's like a giant rotating wardrobe of several hundred cubic metres. The Lightstocks contain about 80 cubic metres, all movable on three axes. Everything is automated and controlled from a single console located at the periphery of the warehouse.

"When we have to cross the Lightstocks to catch young Bronski, it's a bit of a sport. Only a few experienced handlers make it through. In less than a few minutes, the corridor you came down no longer exists. You wanted to turn left, and the only way out was to turn right. I'm telling you, my dear, this is a nightmare."

"I understand," said Victoria, "but it's a low-traffic area, so it's probably our best chance of stopping him safely. Especially since, from your description, there are only two reasons why he could go there. Either he's spotted us, which would take away our element of surprise and probably any chance of catching him, I grant you—or he's coming to pick up an object, and then we know where he's going."

"I agree. But let's flip a coin. Heads, he slips through our fingers. Heads, we have a small chance of catching him. I hate flipping dice."

"To hell with your coin toss," Victoria cut in. "I don't know about you, but I like to make my own luck. I'm sure he hasn't seen us, and it doesn't matter what he's after. John's counting on us to stop this guy, so let's hear it—how do we do it?"

"There are four exits," Archi continued, "and the control console is on the north side. We're heading for the south entrance, which we'll seal once we're inside. That leaves three possible exits for us—two bloodhounds. I suggest we split up. You take the west side, and I'll take the east. All that's left is for us to meet at the north point and grab young Bronski."

"Wait a minute," Victoria interrupted. "If I remember correctly, a few minutes ago, you described my plan as…" Victoria paused the conversation to emphasise her point. "Let me think," she continued. "Oh yes, I remember, 'a lousy plan'. Then you come along, all guns blazing, with a plan in which you want us to cover three possible exits in pairs, dividing our forces to arrive on opposite sides, while our suspect patiently waits for our arrival. I can't find the words to describe your plan."

Archi chuckled slightly at Victoria's impetuous reaction. In that moment, he understood why John had let himself be seduced so easily. She reminded him a little of Isabella, with the same passion and frankness.

"You didn't let me finish, so I can…" Archi insisted in a slightly mocking tone.

Victoria, aware that she had got carried away, would have blushed slightly if her foundation hadn't been so effective.

"Go ahead," she said, unperturbed.

"Very good. His father has been working on Stargraber for years. Young Hubert, on the other hand, has only recently been hired by John. If he's looking for an item, his father must have told him how to retrieve it without going into too much detail. He can only do this near the north door, where there is a control panel that manages the entire warehouse. Also, for security reasons, any movement of the cubicles is signalled by flashing lights all over the warehouse. Then we'll take our chance. It'll take him a few minutes to move the cubic he's interested in. That's exactly how long it will take us to get to him. Once we reach him, you'll take the opportunity to move to his left and get his attention, giving me enough time to come from the right and sneak up behind him to neutralise him.

"You go west, I'll go east. Be careful, when he starts to use the control panel, the cubes will move in a way that makes sense to the computer, but is completely random to us. And therein lies the danger. You can easily get lost, or worse, get run over by a cubic weighing between one and five tonnes. In order for the cubic to get to the control panel, the entire warehouse is set in motion. You literally have to have eyes in the back of your head."

"I may be adventurous by nature, but I'm beginning to wish I'd called John and his men to help us. If I get lost, your whole plan falls apart."

"Don't worry, my dear," Archi resumed with a mannered air. "Didn't I tell you that I've been rubbing shoulders with two gentlemen from maintenance for some time now?"

"No, you didn't," Victoria replied in a similar tone. "They probably play bridge," she added.

"Don't scoff. Those two guys took so much money from me in poker that I stopped seeing them for my sanity. They did, however, teach me how to recognise when the cubes are on the move, and in retrospect, I think the investment was well worth it."

Victoria didn't argue, aware that Archi's pride had been hurt.

"You'll see a virtual compass rose on each cubic," Archi continued. "You'll find one on every visible side. They will show you the upcoming moves, so remember what I'm about to tell you."

"I'm all ears. Go on," Victoria said, clearly attentive.

"The roses aren't there to indicate north. They're there to let you know which cubic will move in which direction."

"I thought as much," Victoria said with a knowing smile. "That seemed far too simple. But I'm listening."

"When a compass rose starts flashing, it means it will move in the next three seconds. Then, the arrows indicating the points of the compass will also begin to flash, showing the direction of movement. Still with me?"

"It's crystal clear," Victoria said, raising her eyebrows.

"Perfect," Archi continued. "Now it gets interesting. The points of the compass indicate right, left, up and down. However, in the context of a warehouse, depth must also be taken into account."

"Of course," Victoria replied, no longer able to smile.

"To find out if a cube is moving towards you or away from you, you use the colour of the cardinal points. Green means it's moving away from you; red means it's your turn to keep your distance."

"I hope you haven't lost too much at poker to know all this! Anyway, thanks. I think I can handle it."

"All right, let's go."

After leaving the hydroponics lab and recovering from his ordeal, John returned to Gerald Bedford's office to report on the failure to arrest Bronski Sr.

"This is unfortunate. Very unfortunate," Bedford yelled at John. "You're my head of security. I thought I could count on you."

"I thought so too, Gerald," John replied. "But as I feared, we had an imponderable. His son had time to warn him of Archi's release, and then everything happened very quickly."

"And what on earth are you doing with this Victoria Palmers?" Bedford continued. "A civilian, to boot. She follows you everywhere, into every corner of the station, and you put her life in danger. If she were a Capsulian, I could live with that, but she's a pure Terran. You know the rules as well as I do. If anything happens to her, both our careers are at stake. The political rivalries between Earth and the station mean we have to be careful. She was originally a VIP guest of the station, wasn't she, John?"

"Yes, I can't deny that," John replied.

"Then I wonder what's going through your head," Bedford continued angrily. "If a VIP on the station cuts his little finger while spreading his bread for breakfast, we've got a diplomatic incident on our hands. So if she's seriously injured or worse, I'll let you imagine the consequences."

John tucked his head into his shoulders and raised his eyebrows slightly but didn't say a word. Bedford watched in amazement. He was used to getting John to react, but at no time had the former Marine behaved like a child caught stealing jam.

After a few seconds of reflection, Bedford's face changed dramatically and softened. He had just understood John's reasons for acting the way he did.

"Don't tell me what I believe, John, please," Bedford said in a more friendly tone.

"Sorry? I don't understand..."

"You have a crush on this girl, I'm sure," Bedford clarified.

John proudly puffed out his chest.

"I think it's deeper than that. Love at first sight would be a more accurate term."

"Coup de foudre, my eye. You're thinking with your pants, my friend," Bedford said, trying to lighten the mood.

"Don't you dare, Gerald," John snapped. "Victoria deserves more respect. And I want her to be part of this investigation; she's intimately involved. Her life has been threatened too, and I think I'd be better able to protect her if I had her close. In a way, she's the one who brought this case to us. If she hadn't come to Stargraber, we probably would have learned too late that there was a dangerous madman on the station who wanted to blow everything up. The Bronskis would have been free to do as they pleased."

Bedford had his answer. John was indeed in love. And nothing would make him give up on keeping Victoria in his immediate circle to protect her. He knew that John was a complete person when it came to feelings. He'd often tried to talk to him about Isabella and share his grief, but he'd been rebuffed far too often to know that John's private life was an inaccessible garden.

"And I don't suppose you have any idea where Mathias Bronski is at the moment?" asked Bedford.

"No. He could be anywhere. But there's still hope we can pick up his trail before he carries out his Machiavellian plan, whatever it may be."

"I'm listening," Bedford said, rising from his desk and taking a few steps around the room to calm his nerves.

"After checking the collectors," John continued, "Archi and Victoria came across the Bronski boy. The last I heard, he was in the bar at the Lunar One. I told them not to take any chances and to pick him up in an unfrequented area."

"And do you have any idea where they are?"

"Not exactly," John replied coyly.

"Explain yourself, John. My sense of humour has reached its limit."

"I haven't heard from them since, and I can't reach them on their Gcom."

"Didn't I just say I'm tired of laughing?" Bedford cut in, annoyed.

"If I can't reach them on their Gcom, then they can only be found in a few very specific places on the station."

"I see," Bedford continued. "If their signal isn't getting through, they must be in a secure area."

"Yes, exactly. A secure area or in the warehouses," John confirmed with a slight chuckle.

"That's all well and good," Bedford said, pacing near his desk, "but we don't have the time or resources to cover every area, let alone search every warehouse."

"The Lunar One restaurant is not far from the Lightstocks warehouse and the armoury. I'm betting they're in one of them, since the moment I lost their signal and the distance between them and those places coincide."

"All right. We have no choice," Bedford said. "Send your men to the most critical areas, and I'll come with you to check out these two rooms. I'll take care of the armoury and leave the Lightstocks to you. I never liked that lab mouse maze."

After keeping a safe distance to avoid detection, Archi and Victoria arrived at the Lightstocks warehouse a few moments after Hubert Bronski.

"Let him go," Archi said, holding Victoria's arm. "We have to wait until he reaches the control panel before we attack. Then we'll know where he is. On the other hand, we'll only have a limited amount of time to reach him."

"How much time exactly?" asked Victoria.

"The warehouse is about 500 cubic metres. Almost an entire module of the station is used here. If Bronski activates the system, it will only take four or five minutes to reach him. That's how long it takes to get the cubic that contains what he came for."

"Five minutes to cover 1,650 feet sounds manageable," Victoria said with a straight face.

"It's harder than it looks," said Archi. "With the cubics on the move, distances can more than double. If we're going to make it, we'll have to get through the warehouse at full speed without getting run over."

He had barely finished his sentence when a siren sounded throughout the warehouse. A distinctive orange rotating beacon indicated that the cubics were about to go into action.

"It's time," Archi shouted, trying to cover the metallic sound of the walls that had just begun to move. "We have less than five minutes, Victoria. See you at the control panel. Good luck."

She had barely finished her sentence when Archi disappeared behind a moving cube. Victoria took a few seconds to analyse the cubics' movements before jumping in. She was stunned by the spectacle before her eyes. The compass roses all seemed to light up at the same time like Christmas lights, and the cubic ballet had nothing to envy of the best Broadway shows.

With no time to spare and no logical way to get around, Victoria took off down the first corridor that came her way. She hadn't gone more than a few feet when the corridor she thought she had entered closed in on her with the sudden arrival of two cubics from opposite directions. They collided with a metallic clang, bringing Victoria to a screeching halt. Her neck twisted 180 degrees in search of a sign that would allow her to avoid turning back.

Suddenly, to her right, she saw a compass rose begin to flash, and the arrow pointing north followed suit. The wall hadn't risen a metre, and Victoria had already slipped underneath it to waste as little time as possible. No sooner had she passed the obstacle than another directional arrow on the cube in front of her indicated that it was about to move to the left. Just enough time to take a few chassé steps to the right, and an opening allowed her to continue forward.

After 300 feet or so, Victoria found her rhythm, anticipating movements like a seasoned handler. The grace of her movements – jumps, rolls, sprints and sudden stops – in the midst of these moving walls weighing thousands of kilos was reminiscent of a choreography in which Victoria was the main character and the cubics a troupe of twirling dancers.

Having covered almost the entire distance to her destination, Victoria paused for a moment to catch her breath. At the same moment, all the cubics stopped simultaneously.

Hubert Bronski turned back to the cube that had just stopped in front of him. He looked for the 139th cube his father had indicated. Fortunately, the cube in question was just to his right. A few more moments – just enough time to dial the secret code and place his thumb on the fingerprint reader – and he would be able to leave this sinister place.

As the cubes stopped moving, the warehouse fell into a deafening silence. Archi and Victoria were forced to tiptoe to the end of their advance. They were now in a position to intervene. Each was hidden behind a corner of the last cubicle where Bronski was working. A metre and a half separated them from their respective targets – a tempting distance for quick action.

Victoria knew Archi wouldn't move until she had young Hubert's attention. As if to give herself courage, she counted backwards before stepping in front of Bronski.

"Who the hell are you?" asked Hubert Bronski, recoiling at the sight of Victoria.

"Sorry," she replied. "I don't think that's any of your business. However, I'm going to need access to the control panel next to you to get to my cubic."

Victoria watched Archibald's arrival with some trepidation, for the man before her was imposing. Despite the few tricks her father had taught her, it was obvious that it would take more than one of them to master this one.

"I'm almost done," Bronski continued, still fiddling with a metal case he'd pulled from the cubic.

Victoria looked over young Hubert's shoulder from time to time. She waddled on the spot, tiptoeing softly, tilting her head from right to left. This almost tribal dance had finally caught Bronski's attention. Victoria's controlled nervousness was palpable throughout the room. Aware of this behaviour she couldn't control, Victoria felt it was time for Archi to intervene.

"It's now or never, Archi," she said to herself, as Hubert Bronski stood up and grabbed the briefcase.

No sooner had she thought these words than Archi appeared behind Hubert, ready to pounce on his target. Meanwhile, Hubert Bronski, who had noticed Victoria's strange behaviour out of the corner of his eye, had instinctively increased his vigilance. He turned his head mechanically to make sure that he and Victoria were indeed alone. Still half hidden by the corner of the cube, Archi appeared to him, almost unreal.

"Now!" Archi shouted at Victoria. Knowing he'd been discovered, he realised that only a spontaneous reflex could save a plan that was beginning to unravel furiously.

The level of adrenaline in Victoria's body rose to such an extent that her alertness increased tenfold, and she felt as if everything were happening in slow motion. With courage on her side, she threw herself violently at Hubert Bronski. The five feet between her and her opponent seemed much larger than they actually were.

As she closed the distance between herself and Bronski, she had time to realise that Archi had followed in the same gesture. Unfortunately, they weren't the only ones with an adrenaline rush. Hubert Bronski's reaction was equally instantaneous. In a fluid movement, he turned on himself and raised his arms like a bullfighter. This had the effect of placing him behind Victoria, who missed her target and landed on the ground facing Archi.

"Don't move, you slugs," Bronski laughed as Victoria and Archi struggled to their feet.

"Wait," Archi tried, looking up at Bronski. "We know about you and your father. You have no chance of escaping the station. You're being actively sought, and every exit is being controlled. Surrender before it's too late."

"Before it's too late for whom?" said Bronski rhetorically, opening the briefcase he was carrying.

As he stood up, Archi put his arm in front of Victoria to pull her behind him. He had recognised the object Bronski was now brandishing and was trying to protect her. John had shown him this type of device on several occasions.

"Yes, Mr Mac Dugan," said the young Bronski, who had met Archi's gaze. "It is a Nox9 remote control. So I suggest you stay very still and let me go without any resistance."

Nox9 was a homemade explosive used during the factional war in which John had participated. It was nicknamed the kamikaze explosive. In a last-ditch effort, the departing factions that were losing the war had the idea to create this fearsome weapon. Undetectable, these explosives had the peculiarity of being connected to their remote controls, which contained more explosives than the bomb itself.

Once the main blast was activated, the remote control, in turn, armed itself to create a second blast even more devastating than the first. This caused considerable damage to the camps of the Allied factions. The undercover men created the first blast in such a way as to move as many people as possible in their direction. When they found themselves among survivors panicked by the first blast, all they had to do was trigger the second blast in a kamikaze fashion to cause as many deaths as possible.

"It's set for manual release," Bronski continued, "so I'm going to my father. If you interfere, I won't hesitate to sacrifice myself for our cause, and my father will be proud of me."

Sensing that young Hubert was very close to his father, Victoria, realising the seriousness of the situation, tried her hand at poker.

"You don't have to do this, Mr Bronski," she said in a very calm tone. "We've already arrested your father. Come with us. You won't get anything out of killing yourself."

"No, no, no," repeated Hubert. "I don't believe you. You can't have arrested him; that's impossible."

"I can assure you that it is quite possible. He's the one who told us where to find you."

Victoria was very convincing. Even Archi, who didn't say a word, was admiring. They could see doubt creeping into Bronski's face. Waving his remote control in the air, Hubert tried to make a call with his Gcom, but no signal came through. Panic began to overtake doubt. The young Bronski began to fidget and think aloud.

"I don't understand," he muttered. "Father had planned it all."

Archi quickly understood what Victoria meant. Knowing Stargraber far better than Victoria, he was on the lookout for any clue Bronski might reveal.

"He knew no one would look for him there. An ideal vantage point," he said unintelligibly. "How, how? I don't believe it. I don't give a damn," continued young Hubert loudly. "I'm going to carry out his plan alone, no matter what it takes."

Archi and Victoria had played their last card, and Bronski continued to threaten them with his remote control as he moved towards the exit. Now, they needed a miracle to stop him from getting killed.

Step by step, as a result of their attempts to reason with young Bronski and his threats against them, Victoria and Archi found themselves on one side of the warehouse exit door and Bronski on the other. Just one more step and Hubert could pull the switch that would put him out of reach forever. Archi couldn't take any chances. A series of explosions of this magnitude would have catastrophic consequences.

With Victoria at her wits' end, the two looked at each other and felt a strong sense of helplessness.

The next thing they knew, the heavy sliding door slammed shut.

"Shit, it's my fault," Archi said angrily. "I should have been faster. John would never have let him get away."

"There was nothing else to do," Victoria replied, turning to Archi. "Second, despite all the good things I think of John, I'm sure he wouldn't have done any better than we did."

Victoria had barely finished her sentence when the warehouse door slid open again. Thinking the worst and feeling helpless, Archi and Victoria took a step back.

The image in front of their eyes left them stunned and smiling at the same time. There, right in front of them, stood John, looking proud and at peace, with the remote in one hand and young Bronski in the other.

Victoria and Archi looked at each other again and could only think of one thing to say:

"For a surprise..."

Chapter Nine
A One Way Trip

Victoria, John and Archi waited patiently for Bedford to return to his office. Gerald Bedford was finishing his interrogation of young Bronski in an adjoining room. Feeling partly responsible for the security breach that had compromised the station, he made it a point of honour to get the son to confess.

Victoria waddled back to her chair, clearly losing patience. Undaunted, she asked the question she'd been itching to ask since her return from the warehouse.

"How on earth did you subdue him?" she asked John excitedly.

"Quite simply," he replied. "Bedford and I decided to check out the most likely places we thought we'd find you. Arriving near the warehouse, I thought it wise to start with the door leading to the control panel. That's when I heard you trying to reason with Bronski. Instead of intervening quickly, I decided to wait until he felt safe. By the time he closed the door, I had slipped in behind him. Thinking that he was alone, his attention waned. All I had to do was deliver a well-placed blow to the back of his neck while grabbing his hand to prevent the bomb from detonating. And that was it," he concluded with a smile.

"I admire your composure," Archi concluded.

Bedford stormed into his office and slammed the door.

"Nothing. I couldn't get anything out of him," Bedford groaned, flailing around. "The little shit wouldn't let go."

"Calm down," said Victoria. "Getting upset won't get us anywhere."

"I agree with you," said John. "But I can see Gerald's point. A few hours ago, we were practically holding them both, and now we're back where we started."

"Not exactly," said Victoria. "We've got one of the two Bronskis, and we've cut their team in half. When you met us at the warehouse, we weren't just trying to reason with the young Bronski. My original idea was to get him to talk without him knowing."

"I agree," Archi continued. "And I thought her diversion was brilliant. Letting him think we'd arrested his father really rattled him."

"Thanks, but it just came to me," she said with a touch of pride.

"That's all very nice," said Gerald, who hadn't stopped pacing his desk. "But would you be so kind as to tell us what he's revealed to you, instead of verbally patting yourself on the back?"

"Actually," Victoria continued, "he didn't teach us much. He mumbled a few words through his teeth, but nothing concrete."

"And you, Archi?" Bedford asked as he continued pacing. "Do you remember anything?"

"Under stress," Archi replied, "I don't remember much, but I do remember him saying that his father had a fallback base or something."

"It's thin," said John, searching for what these meagre clues might correspond to. "Victoria," he continued, "if I may take you aside, I'd like to try something."

"We can stay, or we can bother you," Archi remarked sarcastically.

"Very funny," John replied, taking Victoria to a corner of the room.

John sat across from Victoria and held her hands.

"I'm going to try to help you get back into the situation so you can access your memories more easily. Maybe you'll remember something that will put us on the right track."

"I didn't know you were a hypnotist," Victoria said.

"You'll be conscious throughout this exercise. The goal is to see your memories from a different perspective, so that every detail comes back to you. Now relax and close your eyes."

Victoria did as she was told, comforted by the warmth radiating from John's palms.

"Good, that's very good," John said as he felt Victoria's hands relax between his. "Now remember. What did you see when Bronski began to speak? Describe the situation to me at that exact moment."

"I can only see the remote control for the bomb in his hand," she replied. "Everything else is a blur."

"What do you hear?" John continued.

"I can hear him mumbling, but it's very far away."

"How do you feel?"

"I'm hot, and at the same time, I can feel my whole body shaking."

"Do you remember a particular smell at that moment?"

"Yes, a pungent smell, but I can't define it."

"That's okay. But can you associate that smell with a taste?" John continued.

"Yes, yes. I've smelt that in a gallery on Earth. It's sulphur. My mouth tastes like sulphur," said Victoria, her face lighting up as she discovered all these forgotten sensations.

"That's very good. Hold this moment and stay focused. Keep your eyes closed. Now, the image of Bronski holding the remote control — do you see it in colour or black and white?"

"It's in black and white."

"That's normal — a bad memory is often perceived in monochrome. Can you try to make it a colour one?"

"I'll try," Victoria replied, frowning in concentration.

"Now, I'd like you to change the angle of this picture, and try to rotate it as if you were turning around Bronski and his remote control."

"That's it," said Victoria. "That's fun. I feel like there's less remote control, and Bronski is less intimidating. I can see him from above. The picture seems to clear up."

"Perfect," John continued, clearly admiring Victoria's ability to express her emotions. "Keep moving around in this picture and find a distance between you and Bronski that will allow you to hear him more clearly. I'm all ears."

Victoria, whose face had calmed down, was still struggling to find the right distance. You could follow her intellectual progress by watching her head move. Her fear of Bronski forced her to concentrate. John could see numerous eye movements through her eyelids.

"I've got it," Victoria said suddenly, opening her eyes. "I can hear him now. He said his father had done away with everything, but he didn't say what. Then he said that his father had an ideal point of view, but he didn't say anything about a home base. I'm not quite sure what that means, but that's what he said."

"That doesn't get us very far," said Bedford, who had stopped pacing during the session. "I know the station well, but the only time

I get a good view is from my office when my secretary brings me my morning coffee."

"Very funny," said Archi. "But if that doesn't tell you anything, then we're right back where we started, and the station is still under threat. What do you think, John?"

"I'm thinking," he said, rising from his chair. "I was wondering why young Bronski, who obviously has suicidal tendencies, didn't take the opportunity to blow us all up. If his and his father's goal was to destroy Stargraber, they had two golden opportunities. When Bronski Sr blew up part of the research centre's canopy, he should have blown up the airlocks to weaken the station's structure. We'd have had a hard time containing the cascade of decompressions that would have brought down the station sooner or later. Similarly, the young Bronski threatens us and tries to escape instead of destroying us. I've come to believe that their goal may not be to destroy Stargraber."

"Your analysis makes sense," Victoria said. "But if you're right, we're even more lost than we were a minute ago. All of our actions have been based on the premise that Stargraber is under threat. Now, we don't even know what the Bronskis want — or where Mathias is."

Bedford had resumed his incessant pacing, Archi held his head in his hands to think more clearly, and John and Victoria stood facing a porthole, scanning the stars in the hope of seeing more clearly. A heavy silence fell over the room.

After a minute, John, still facing the porthole, interrupted the impromptu brainstorming.

"Has anyone recovered the information collector we had the Bronskis analyse?"

"I'm sorry," Bedford said.

"Yes, when young Bronski brought you the results, did he also give you the data collector?"

"Yes, indeed," replied Bedford. "It must be here in my office. I didn't take the time to get rid of it. We were looking for Archi at the time."

"I see what you're getting at, John," Archi continued. "Your idea is excellent. With a little luck, Bronski may have forgotten to delete certain information. Give it to me, Gerald, and I'll have a look at it right away."

Bedford handed the collector to Archi, who placed it on the desk to interface with the mainframe. In less than a second, the virtual keyboard appeared, along with a message: *Module ready for initialisation.*

The only word that came to Archi's mind at that moment was: "Shit."

"What the hell?" Bedford muttered.

"Shit. That means this collector is completely empty. It never contained any information. It's just formatted to make us think it's authentic. Bronski probably destroyed the original and replaced it with this."

"As I was saying," Victoria said, "we're getting nowhere. My mind is as empty as this computer."

"Yes, that's it!" exclaimed John, turning around. "That's the second time today you've been brilliant."

"Can you power our LEDs?" asked Bedford.

"I'm no computer scientist," John continued, "but all these collectors look alike. In his haste, Gerald hadn't noticed that young Bronski hadn't given him the original."

"Indeed," Archi cut in, "but what's so great about Victoria?"

"Well," John continued, "for Mathias Bronski to realise that we were onto him, he either had to physically recognise the collector — and they all look alike — or he had to know what was inside. To do that, he had to use the mainframe, and it may not be as empty as Victoria thinks."

"That's a great idea," Archi said, impressed. "But this information is almost inseparable from the gigantic flood of data contained in the central memory. I may be a scientist, but I don't know anyone on this station who could pull off such a feat."

John looked at Victoria with a wry smile.

"No one on this station," John said to Archi, "I agree with you. However, we know someone who can."

"Jacky!" Archi shouted with a smile.

"I just hope I'll be able to convince him to come to the station. After all, it could be a one-way trip."

Chapter Ten

A Happy Life

The tarmac at the station was busy. John passed two stewardesses who were obviously upset about their last trip. He now knew for certain that Jacky was on board. What bothered him most was that, sooner or later, he would have to keep the promise he had made to Jacky to have him painted on Stargraber.

Since commuters usually used the elevators in the one-legged modules, the arrival of a shuttle was often considered a minor event. Only a few dignitaries, VIPs or influential members of the station used the shuttles. All eyes turned mechanically to Jacky as he stepped out of the shuttle.

Jacky, clearly proud of the small impact he had made, puffed out his chest and called out to John as he approached his friend.

"Johnny, my friend, I don't know why you brought me to your tin can in orbit, but all those pretty almond eyes pointed at me, and the promise you made was well worth the detour. I wonder if I don't have an opening," he added, pointing discreetly at one of the shuttle's hostesses.

"We'll talk about that later, if you like. I need your help now. Follow me."

"Wow, you look so serious, like the fate of mankind is at stake."

"I don't know, Jacky, but I hope you can tell me," said John as he walked towards a departing sailboat.

"Man," said Jacky, following in his friend's footsteps, "I probably should have asked for more."

Archi and Victoria anxiously awaited John's return. Each of them tried to understand what the motives and goals of the Bronski family might be. Archi couldn't bring himself to believe that Mathias Bronski could elude them. Victoria, for her part, felt that the situation did not look good. She had only gotten involved by accident. Her mining experience was useless on a space station. Only her encounter with John made her smile, but the prospect of losing her life prevented her from projecting herself into any kind of future.

When the door to Archi's office opened, Victoria was startled from her thoughts. She recognised Jacky, and a feeling of hope came over her. Maybe he would give them the answers they needed.

"Archi, good to see you again," Jacky called as he walked over to his friend. "Hello, beautiful lady," he said as he passed Victoria.

"I see you haven't changed, you old satyr," Archi replied, giving him a manly hug.

"Then I'm needed," Jacky continued, looking around the room. "Will one of you finally fill me in?"

"When Victoria and I came to you," John said, "we were looking for information about a certain Buba Kellnik."

"I remember."

"We were under the mistaken impression that he was after us. We later discovered that we were dealing with a saboteur on the station. Long story short, we know his name, he knows we're after him, but we don't know his true intentions or where he is. We're counting on you to tell us."

"He's a madman with a crazy son," Archi said. "He had me kidnapped by his offspring and tried to suppress John by banishing him into space."

"And you know nothing else? No threats, no demands?"

"No, Jacky," John continued. "We captured his son, but the only things he was willing to say led us to believe that he had a precise plan and great determination. His name is Mathias Bronski."

"Unknown," said Jacky.

"We discovered his identity," John continued, giving him information to analyse. "It was in this data collector. Unfortunately, it's empty, reformatted as new."

"I see," Jacky cut in. "I know why you need me. All those brain-dead people in the core couldn't find the data that Bronski had to analyse with the help of your mainframe to find out what was in that collector."

"Right, and thanks for the compliment," Archi snapped.

"Don't take it personally, my friend. I was just pointing out that you live in a pre-formatted universe. As soon as you need to do some in-depth research, your overly specific qualifications get in the way, that's all."

"Speak for yourself, dear friend," Victoria snapped. "I feel perfectly competent in my field, and I know how to adapt when necessary. My presence among you is proof of that."

"That's all well and good," said John, obviously used to Jacky's wild theories, "but if we could be more constructive, I think we could all benefit."

"Okay, Johnny, I'm on it," Jacky said, taking a seat behind Archi's desk. "Hand me the collector, please."

"It's no use to you, it's completely empty," Archi pointed out.

"I'll just use it as a starting point to track down your suspect. The formatting number will tell me where to look."

After several minutes of manipulation, Jacky stopped. Every member of the team hung on his nimble fingers. Then he resumed his obsessed posture, which no one envied him for, making the grimaces he regularly made in spite of himself.

"I've got something," Jacky said calmly. "It was well disguised, but thanks to your friend Jacky, he's hit the jackpot."

"Spare us your unique sense of humour," said John, "and let us enjoy your find instead."

"Very good. All this information relates to terrestrial geological studies. I don't have the complete data, but this is seismological data. All of this information was collected over a period of about three months."

"That's about the same time young Bronski was hired at the lab," Archi noted.

"All the stored data correspond to micro-earthquakes," Jacky continued, "at a rate of about two per month."

"I can confirm that information," said Victoria. "Over the past few months, our mines have been regularly shaken, especially since these tremors have been accompanied by heat waves that have almost cost the lives of several of my employees."

"We've already investigated that hypothesis," John interrupted. "It suggested that Bronski was using energy flows from overloads generated by the station to create these heat waves. Overloading all the one-legged modules would create a chain reaction capable of destroying the station. However, to do that, he would have to affect all the one-legged modules on Stargraber at the same time, which is unlikely, if not impossible."

"Wait a minute," said Jacky, who looked distraught. "You assumed Bronski was going to attack the station." He paused. "And if you were thinking on a larger scale," he went on.

"There's every reason to believe that," Archi insisted, sounding annoyed. "Hubert Bronski made it clear how much his father hated Stargraber. What could be more important? Earth?" he added with a sneer.

A heavy silence fell over the room. Only Archi's laughter echoed through the space. Victoria, realising the meaning of that word before anyone else, felt a sudden urge to sit down. Archi, resting one hand on the wall so as not to lose his balance, imagined the magnitude of his proposal.

"But how?" asked John, looking serious as he broke the silence.

"With a chain reaction," Jacky replied, "just like you imagined for Stargraber, but aimed at Earth. In a way, I'm surprised you didn't make the connection sooner, Miss Palmers. After the Big One of 2112, new fault lines formed along the new coast from New Mexico to Wyoming. Along the way, they created what we call the Afterones, the galleries that are your source of income, sweetheart."

"I see what you're getting at, Jacky," Archi interrupted doubtfully, "but I still don't get it. In my opinion, it can only cause a low-intensity earthquake. The new faults were created recently and are stable. Add to that draconian building standards, and the damage would be minimal."

"Yes, I agree with you," said Jacky. "That's why I asked you to think bigger."

Victoria, John and Archi looked at each other in palpable disbelief. They all expected and feared Jacky's conclusion.

"He doesn't want to create an earthquake," Jacky continued. "He wants to create a volcanic eruption!"

For a moment, only the sound of the air conditioner could be heard as everyone tried to make up their minds. Suddenly, everyone was shouting at the same time, trying to undermine this proposal, which they considered far-fetched at best.

"You can't be serious," John said in a tone that silenced the rest of the group. "First of all, what volcano are you talking about?"

"Yellowstone, that's obvious. He wants to blow up Yellowstone."

The commotion started again.

"Quiet," Jacky called to his comrades, "I'll tell you how Bronski plans to do it."

Everyone fell silent again.

"The micro-earthquakes and heat waves Bronski was creating occurred on precise dates. They set the stage for D-Day. Over time, Bronski weakened the Earth's crust in preparation for his final attack. The Afterones are so extensive that they run from the coastal faults to Yellowstone. The barrier separating the Afterones from the volcano is very thin. It owes its stability to the fact that Yellowstone is so vast. When the volcano is at rest, the relative pressure generated by the magma equilibrates with the atmospheric pressure in the vents.

"If Mathias builds up enough energy in his next attempt, he will break through the barrier that separates the Afterones from the Yellowstone volcano. The heat wave generated by the station to create the earthquake will follow a few minutes later. This intense heat will be enough to raise the temperature of the volcanic chamber significantly. The result of this sudden rise in temperature will be a build-up of pressure in the volcanic chamber that will inevitably cause one of the world's largest volcanoes to explode. I will leave you to imagine the consequences."

"That's just it," Victoria said. "I'd like to know what the effects of such an eruption would be."

"A super-eruption like this," Archi replied, "would have worldwide repercussions. Yellowstone has had three major eruptions in its history. The last one occurred about 640,000 years ago. It was 3,000 times more powerful than the eruption of Mount Vesuvius and was responsible for the mass extinction of many species of life in the Americas. Since that last eruption, the volcano's magma chamber has been recharging. Each year that passes brings us closer to another major eruption.

"In our case, Bronski wants to trigger an explosion of the volcano and combine it with an earthquake, thus greatly increasing the effects of a simple eruption."

"But you still haven't told us what to expect," Victoria worried again.

"First of all," Archi continued gravely, "within a radius of nearly 60 miles, all life will be destroyed by fiery clouds of molten dust, rock and lava reaching speeds of nearly 310 miles per hour, combined with infernal temperatures of around a thousand degrees.

"Beyond 60 miles, volcanic ash up to 25 inches thick will cause most buildings to collapse. In a conventional eruption, only six inches is enough to collapse the roof of a house. I leave you to imagine what will happen in our major cities. All skyscrapers have been built to strict seismic standards, but none of them are designed to withstand significant pressure from above. If their structures can't withstand it, they will collapse like houses of cards.

"Of course, the world's airways will be paralysed by the ash cloud. The same ash will contaminate all the world's drinking water supplies with sulphuric acid. It will also reach the stratosphere to change the entire climate. I'll spare you the details of the fluorosis and other lung diseases that will be caused in the coming months.

"Everything I've just described, in quotes, would be the result of a normal eruption. The addition of a seismic tremor would multiply the consequences by a factor I don't know and dare not imagine."

"That's it," Victoria mumbled. "I'm officially scared."

"I understand," John said, taking Victoria in his arms to reassure her. "I'm going to do everything in my power to stop this man. Whatever his reasons, they will never justify genocide in my eyes."

"Maybe so," Archi added, "but until we know where he's hiding, all our talk is useless."

"Jacky," John said, "maybe you can help us narrow down our search."

"I'm a computer genius," he replied, examining his fingernails, "not a magician. If you don't give me a minimum of clues, there's nothing I can do."

"Exactly," said Victoria. "We are looking for a place with an ideal vantage point from which we can keep an infallible watch on the surroundings. This is all we've got, so I hope it'll do."

"Give me a few minutes," Jacky said, leaning back over the desk.

"In the meantime," John said, "Victoria and I will keep Bedford informed. As soon as Jacky has any news, meet us at the security centre. Don't use your Gcoms; I suspect Bronski has bugged us, or at least I would have, so there is no radio communication."

Fifteen minutes later, Bedford emerged from his office accompanied by Victoria and John.

"I'm telling you, John," he said in a tone that did not invite discussion, "Little California is the scene of a terrorist attack, and with no news of your friend, I have no choice but to seal off the station."

"That's a mistake, sir," John replied categorically. "If Bronski feels cornered and we haven't located him, he will carry out his plan and disappear. We may not be able to stop this programmed disaster."

"Give them a few more minutes," Victoria added. "Jacky was really helpful in uncovering the Bronskis' plan."

"I'm sorry," Bedford replied, "but from what you've told me, the one-legged module will release an enormous amount of energy. No one, not even Archi, can tell what effect that will have on Stargraber. I'm forced to evacuate Little California to the Russian and European modules."

No sooner had he finished his sentence than he activated the station's alarm system. A discreet signal sounded, and every panel in every room and corridor relayed the same message: "Alert, evacuation in progress."

Within moments, Stargraber had become a veritable anthill fleeing a flood. Every member of every section knew what to do. The evacuation began with apparent calm. Everyone carried a single backpack filled with what was important to them. The station now resembled a pressure cooker ready to explode. Its inhabitants acted like steam, trying to escape as quickly as possible.

Messages broadcast throughout the station instructed everyone to use the only two navigators still functioning to reach the modules of neighbouring nations. However, as with any evacuation, panic gripped the less prepared, and many untrained commuters formed crowds around the Navigon entrances. This situation forced residents to find alternative routes. As a last resort, the escape pods were also taken by storm.

Bedford, accompanied by Victoria and John, gave final evacuation instructions to the few stragglers they encountered.

"Still no word," Victoria announced as she pointed out the nearest exit to a visibly lost kitchen assistant.

"Nothing on my end," Bedford replied from a nearby corridor.

"I think I see them," John called out between shoves.

The next moment, Jacky and Archi appeared at John's side in a corridor that seemed narrower than usual under the circumstances. Nevertheless, a semblance of calm began to settle. John took the opportunity to invite the group to join him in the break room for an update on the situation.

"This place has never been more aptly named," Jacky tried to lighten the mood.

"But what's going on?" said Archi. "We had to locate Bronski without his knowledge in order to neutralise him. Now he knows without a doubt that we're actively looking for him. He must also suspect that we have his son."

"I decided to evacuate the station and young Hubert," Bedford replied. "Since no one was in a position to determine the consequences of Bronski's attack on the station, I was obliged to protect its population."

"I know what you mean," said John. "In fact, I think it's a good decision, one that could be useful to us."

"I don't mean to be negative," Victoria continued, "but we're the only ones left on the station, so how is that going to help us?"

"Because he's the only one left to look for," Jacky said in his usual humorous tone.

"Exactly," John continued, giving his friend a friendly pat on the shoulder. "He's on his own. We have his son, and he's made it clear that he's determined to carry out his plan. The evacuation of the station will isolate him. Jacky will be in charge of tracking him with the station's sensors. Once we know where he's hiding, we can take action and try to stop this madness."

"To locate him," Jacky interrupted, tapping on the virtual keyboard in the break room, "I need direct access to the central server. Bronski controls a large part of the computer system. If we're going to stop him, I need to get part of the system back. I'm leaving right now, but I need you, Bedford."

"How can I help you?"

"Your level one access codes should still work, so we can get to the heart of the system. You're coming with me."

"What if he's already there?" Victoria cut in.

"Not to worry," Jacky replied. "The system was too difficult to access. Bronski was only able to hack into part of it from the outside, just enough to carry out his plan."

"Very well," said John. "Go ahead. In the meantime, I'm going to the observatory. It's the only place I can think of that's a central point with an excellent vantage point and several exits. If I'm lucky, I'll find Bronski there; if not, it's a central location from which I can intervene quickly."

"Perfect, we'll go with you," said Victoria and Archi in unison.

"Out of the question," John cut in sharply. "This guy is much too dangerous. I don't want to take any risks if we don't have to."

"But you're not going alone," Victoria worried.

"Don't worry. Once I've located him, Bedford and Jacky will come and support me. And I'll point out that he's also alone and a civilian. His plan is ruthless, I grant you, but he has no training."

"Besides," Bedford added, "within the hour, this place will be swarming with men from every government agency with at least three letters in it."

"Meanwhile," John continued, "I want to catch the bastard who tried to shoot me into space."

As Jacky and Bedford left for the central server, John took Archi by the arm to speak to him in passing.

"Archi, I need you here. I need you to protect Victoria."

"Don't worry, my friend, I'll take her down in the next elevator."

"That's out of the question. We didn't evacuate thousands of people to neighbouring stations via the Navigons just for fun. The elevators were shut down as soon as the evacuation began. Bedford told me there are two shuttles left on the tarmac. Take one with Victoria and stay in low orbit until it's all over. I don't want her on Stargraber or Earth for another minute."

"I understand. But beware of Bronski. This man is of the vicious and calculating breed. They're the most dangerous," Archi concluded, shaking hands with his friend.

"One last thing," John continued, "can you give me two minutes alone with Victoria? I want to talk to her."

Archi complied and left the room immediately. John turned to Victoria and moved closer so he could smell her light yet intoxicating perfume.

"I'm sorry, Vicky, we haven't had a chance to talk since we kissed. I just—"

Victoria interrupted him by placing her index finger in front of John's lips.

"Don't say another word. I know what you were going to say. Blame it on my feminine intuition, but if I'm as worried about you as you are about me, it's probably because I feel the same way you do. I'd prefer it if we could talk about this when we're past it, because I think once we start talking, I might revert to my teenage self and want it to get us through the night, and the next, and the next."

Victoria wore her most beautiful smile. John could only stare at her, enchanted. Once again, she had anticipated his intentions. He thought he was reassuring her by doing his job as a man, but in the end, it was he who felt more confident letting her go with Archi.

To drive the point home, Victoria delicately placed her lips on his. This time, they weren't between elevators, nor did they have to put on an act to convince a friend. The moment their kiss became more intimate, John understood the magnitude of the words Victoria had just spoken. His mind could no longer distinguish between pleasure and reason.

For the first time in a very long time, he had completely surrendered. He was now sure of one thing, and that was that if he managed to come out of this affair unscathed, there was only one outcome waiting for him: a happy life.

Chapter Eleven
This Could Be the End

John had just arrived at the observatory. It was a popular spot for children during the day and for teenagers after dark. After the noisy evacuation of the station, John knew that radio silence was no longer an option. In any case, he needed Jacky to lead him back to Bronski. John had to take the risk that he had been bugged. He put his wrist to his ear to activate his Gcom.

"Jacky, where are you? I've just arrived at the observatory. I'm going to go in and take a look around."

"The detectors will be ready in a few minutes," Jacky said. "Bronski did more damage than expected. So be careful, we still don't know where he is."

"Yes, Moman," John answered sarcastically. "I'm going to take a look around the observatory until Archi contacts me to confirm that Victoria is safely aboard the shuttle. As for you, call me as soon as you've located this dangerous lunatic."

Archi and Victoria were only a few steps away from the hangar.

"Victoria," Archi said, "are you relieved that this story is over?"

"I will be when we all have a good drink," she replied.

"I don't blame you, but I trust John. Even if Bronski is a psychopath, I know he won't take any chances unless he absolutely has to."

"That's what I'm afraid of," Victoria said, nodding. "When you're dealing with someone who's disturbed, your bearings are often challenged, and you may not be true to your principles."

"John has always been faithful in everything since I've known him," Archi pointed out.

"You say that for me," Victoria said. "You know, there's nothing serious between us yet. I think the context has brought us together faster than expected, but it could all end tomorrow."

"Did John tell you that he's married?" asked Archi.

"No, I didn't know, but we didn't have much time to talk about our lives."

"Her name was Isabella, and her death was a real tragedy for John."

"If I had known, I would have..."

"I didn't want to scare you," Archi interrupted. "I just wanted you to understand that John doesn't make commitments lightly and to tell you how lucky you are. He's a good man."

"I have received you well. I have principles of my own that I like to uphold. I want to assure you that I won't let him suffer because of me."

"Here we are," Archi interrupted again. "Stay behind me. I prefer to err on the side of caution and, above all, to uphold my principles as a gentleman," he added with a smile.

Archi stepped onto the tarmac, took a few steps, looked to his right and then to his left. Since the flight deck had been evacuated, it took Archi only a few seconds to take in the whole scene. However, the runway and its surroundings were plunged into darkness, with only the emergency lights to guide him.

The dim light intensified the feeling of being in orbit. The gaping opening through which the shuttles left the station was protected only by a force field. Archi felt like he was already in the vacuum of space. He had to check the condition of the shuttles before loading his passenger. Knowing that he was alone, he invited her to follow him.

It took Victoria a few seconds to follow. Archi had already walked several feet towards the two remaining shuttles when Victoria stepped into the doorway. The door had not yet closed when a violent explosion threw Victoria back into the corridor she had just entered.

Disoriented and unable to comprehend what had happened, Victoria struggled to her feet, still dazed from the shock. Her first instinct was to worry about Archi's health. Meanwhile, the automatic security system had sealed off all access to the hangars.

Despite her aching limbs, Victoria reached the porthole of the door she had just passed through. The sight in front of her caused her to let out a scream of horror that she couldn't stop, even though she put her hands over her mouth.

An explosion had damaged the two remaining shuttles and almost the entire runway. The force field was still active but showing signs of weakness. The worst was only a few feet ahead of her, and she had no way to intervene. The smoke from the multiple fires was all heading for a specific point in the hangar.

The explosion had damaged the station's structure, and slow decompression was underway. There were only a few minutes left before the runway would be deprived of all oxygen.

Archi lay on what was left of the floor. He was unconscious, and his left shoulder was pierced by a metal crossbar that prevented him from moving.

A distraught Victoria tried to call for help, but the blast had damaged all peripheral systems and her Gcom. She was helpless.

To add insult to injury, Archi regained consciousness for a few moments. His only reflex was to turn his head toward the door to see if Victoria was safe. When he saw her behind the porthole, he smiled to reassure her.

Victoria was not fooled and returned the smile, but uncontrollable tears began to roll down her cheeks. The emotion was so strong that she was forced to make terrible efforts to keep her legs moving and maintain eye contact with Archi.

The flood of tears intensified. Archi found it harder and harder to breathe. Coughing fits, caused by the blood beginning to fill his lungs, made his shoulder ache intensely.

The sight was unbearable, but Victoria didn't take her eyes off him. She kept eye contact with Archi until he closed his eyes again.

Victoria collapsed at the foot of the sealed door. She realised that Archi would never open his eyes again.

John had stopped in the centre of the observatory's dome, admiring the spectacle of the starry vault. This brief moment of peace was interrupted by a strong vibration beneath his feet. At the same time, his Gcom rang.

"Yes, I'm listening," he said, his head still in the stars.

"It's me," Jacky replied. "The detectors are finally under my control, and you'll never guess where Bronski is."

"No idea. Maybe behind me," replied John, turning around in a fit of conscience.

"Not quite," Jacky continued, "but in a way, he's close to you."

"Go ahead and give birth, Jacky. We haven't got all night."

"All right, I'll give you this: Bronski is in your quarters."

"Where?" John repeated.

"He's in your apartment, and that's not all. As soon as the sensors were back online, Bronski sent me a message on the terminal, asking you to join him. Apparently, he wants to talk to you—perhaps to negotiate his surrender."

"Given his character, I'd be very surprised," John replied. "Thank you for your efficiency. I'm going to leave, but I want you to keep an eye on me. Can you do that?"

"I only control 50% of the system, but I'll do my best. As for my performance, I doubt I can take credit for it. Bronski's call came too close to the moment I regained control. He's playing with us."

"By the way, I felt a big vibration. Did you feel it?"

"It's probably an automatic oil change," John replied. "It happens all the time. I'm going to see Bronski."

As he approached his quarters, John checked his pistol one last time. A few feet from his front door, he slowed down and instinctively checked to make sure he wasn't being followed. The door to his apartment was ajar. He hesitated for a second before pushing it open, knowing his enemy was behind it.

"Come in, Mr Desmond," Mathias Bronski told him in a calm, confident tone, "and make yourself at home."

John walked slowly towards him. Bronski stood in the middle of what had once been John's living room. Now, the place looked more like an aircraft cockpit after a crash. Bronski faced John, surrounded by a battery of screens, all connected by countless cables to interactive panels on the walls of the apartment, whose partitions had been torn open.

A strange iridescent blue glow surrounded Bronski and his equipment. It was as if he were inside a giant soap bubble.

John drew his gun and pointed it at Bronski without saying a word.

"Your gun won't do any good, John," Bronski said, continuing to work on his screens. "I've created a force field to protect me from any aggression, and I love the colour, don't you? Right now, I just want to talk to you."

John, assessing the situation, didn't answer. He was just wondering how he was going to get around his opponent's defences and stop him.

"Let's relax for a moment and talk," Bronski continued. "There's nothing you can do. I assure you there isn't," he added, as John's eyes took in every detail of his installation.

Bronski seemed sure of himself, which had a way of annoying John. His insides were boiling, but he had to face the fact that there was nothing he could do right now except listen to Mathias rant on. Maybe he could even get some useful information by provoking him.

"If I've asked you here, John," Bronski continued, "it's not to try to win you over to my cause, but I want you to understand the importance of what I'm doing."

"You haven't told me anything yet," John replied, sheathing his gun. "Yet you're already expressing yourself like all the madmen who have tried in vain to take over the world."

"Don't be unpleasant. I have no desire to rule the planet. In fact, it's the healthiest it's been in centuries. We use non-polluting energy, all our waste is recycled, and our production is controlled so that it has no impact on the environment. In fact, according to a recent study, our air quality is better than it was during the time of the dinosaurs. No, my dear friend, the planet has nothing to fear from me."

"Is that why you want to blow up a volcano?" interrupted John curtly.

"I see you've done your homework," Bronski replied calmly. "I'm not surprised. You've managed to waste quite a bit of my time over the past few days. But it is still my intention to clean up the planet."

"And you tell me these aren't the words of a madman."

"Don't call me crazy until you've heard me out, Mr Desmond. What I want to accomplish is far more complex than a simple eruption, even on this scale. I want to save humanity from itself, John. I want to give them a chance. I want to do what our leaders are no longer capable of: make drastic decisions. Do you know where we are, John?"

"Is this a trick question?" replied John, a little surprised.

"Let me tell you. We're on a space station built by international cooperation for the benefit of mankind. A station capable of providing an infinite amount of free energy to the entire Earth."

"I agree with you. It's an invention that has united all the peoples of the world under the same banner, putting an end to famine and war. Stargraber has even effectively regulated inequalities between individuals, giving everyone a chance to realise their full potential. Thanks to this station and the free energy it provides, humanity has never been more advanced."

"Do you really think so? Listening to you, it's like listening to a well-crafted political speech. Let me prove you wrong. Originally, before it became Stargraber, the International Space Station was designed to give mankind access to the universe. It was to be a stepping stone to a cosmos full of promise. At that time, mankind was still thirsty for adventure and discovery. Man was still free to imagine his future.

"But in reality, Stargraber only succeeded in enslaving humanity. The economic and political needs of the time quickly slowed the development of interplanetary travel. The failure of Mars One sounded the death knell for the conquest of space. So we retreated to the ISS in Earth orbit. The development of Stargraber was certainly less ambitious than the conquest of the universe, but we thought it was a project capable of advancing our understanding of the space that surrounds us, and above all, a project within our budgetary means at the time."

"And here we are," John cut in, "look around you."

"Yes, we did it, but what's next?"And then what?"Where is mankind going, Mr Desmond? What's the next step in its evolution?"

"I don't know, but why question our way of life? We live in peace and progress at our own pace."

"No, we're not progressing any more. Humanity is dying. Take a good look at the world today, take a good look around you. Take a good look at the way you live. You spend your time in a tin can that has only one purpose: to produce free energy. I challenge you to name one major advance that has taken place in the last fifty years. Free energy should have enabled us to resume the conquest of space, but it has plunged us into a gentle lethargy. Comfortable in his slippers, man has lost his desire to surpass himself.

"Everything is done to make his life easier, but he no longer has free will. The only choice left to him is to go with the flow, without making waves, without expressing his ideas for fear of alienating a certain community. If he is resourceful and tries to go a different way, he is ostracised. If he's better than the others, he's put in his place.

"I'm not talking about the top athletes or Nobel Prize winners who are perfectly integrated into our system, I'm talking about the creative people, the dreamers who used to work in their garages after hours. These people have disappeared from our sanitised environment. Everything is automated and formatted to fit into precise boxes. Excessive equality between individuals has only hastened humanity's downfall.

"I want to give humanity a chance to evolve again. I want a new society to develop on solid foundations, thanks to pioneers with the will to rediscover the wonders that surround them. People are capable of inventing their own future. I want the best to teach the less experienced. I want accidents to happen without necessarily pointing the finger of blame. Death exists, Mr Desmond. I want man to face his demons again, to surpass himself and to rediscover, as he has long done, the desire to make new discoveries.

"More simply, I hope that man will rediscover his zest for life, Mr Desmond."

"May I ask where you expect to find these pioneers so dear to your megalomaniacal project?"

"Right here," Bronski answered. "The people who chose to live on this station did so to find an escape from a life that didn't suit them. Even if some of them did it unconsciously."

"That's all well and good, but even if I agree with you on certain points, I cannot follow you down a path that will lead to the destruction of almost the entire human race. That's genocide, and I will do everything in my power to stop you."

"It's not genocide; it's a necessity. The latest studies show that population growth is constantly increasing. In less than a century, the Earth will no longer be able to support humanity. Despite all the energy we produce, no matter how clean, we won't be able to find a place for everyone. Parked in confined spaces, we'll lose the will to live.

"Free energy has imprisoned man in a torpor that leads to his downfall. He no longer has to fight to get what he wants. His natural urge to conquer the world around him has been suppressed. The very foundations of the human race are threatened, so we must act and purify our population. I'm the only one who realises this, but soon the whole world will.

"Within 40 minutes, the energy capacitor of the American one-legged module will overload, releasing enough energy to trigger the eruption of Yellowstone. Of course, the reason I'm talking so freely about this is that the series of reactions leading to the capacitor overload has already occurred, and no one, not even yours truly, can stop it from happening now."

"That won't stop me from trying to stop you," John said, drawing his gun again.

He adjusted his weapon and fired without warning in the direction of the power cable. The bullet bounced off the force field and embedded itself in the false ceiling of the apartment.

"I told you nothing could stop me. I'm sorry you didn't side with reason. So, I will pursue my destiny alone."

"I'm not done with you yet, Bronski. Once I stop your infernal system, I'll make sure you can't do it again. I'm still convinced there are other ways to achieve the result you seek. I'm not going to let you kill ten billion people to prove a theory."

"To save the world, John. Consider my action an act of war to defend our values and save the world. Human extinction is inevitable. I'm just moving the date up a little bit, trying to save the best part. I don't see myself as a new messiah, but I can save what's left of humanity in all of us."

"People find solutions, Mr Bronski, and I assure you I'll find one to stop you."

"That's what I love about you. That fighting spirit that the rest of you lack. Even when you reach a dead end, you don't give up. Leave me now, I have much to do."

With that, and seeing that there was nothing more he could do by staying there, John backed out of the apartment. Arriving in the hallway, he headed for the computer room to get back to Jacky as quickly as possible.

Walking at a determined pace, he tried to contact Archi and Victoria on their Gcom. When he received no response, he quickened his pace to catch up with Jacky.

For the first time, a feeling of fear came over him. Bronski's plan seemed to be perfect, and his force field would protect him long enough to achieve his goal. He couldn't count on the help of the authorities either – they would obviously arrive too late.

He had to find a way to act quickly, but he had so little room for manoeuvre that he found himself thinking:

This could be the end.

Chapter Twelve

Resigned to the end.

Arriving at the technical centre, John rushed to the computer room where Jacky and Bedford were.

In the corridor leading to the computers, John was overcome by a strange feeling. He was sure he could smell Victoria's distinctive perfume. As he walked on, he dismissed the idea that Victoria could still be on the station. He thought his mind was playing tricks on him.

As the situation worsened, John wondered if he'd been wrong to send Victoria and Archi away from the station. After his conversation with Mathias Bronski, John knew Bronski was going to follow through with his madness. He was worried, and would have preferred Archi and Victoria to be with him to face the situation.

John's surprise was lessened when he entered the computer room. His senses had not betrayed him. Victoria was there, accompanied by Jacky and Bedford. But the excitement of seeing

Victoria was soon replaced by questions. She looked deeply distressed.

"What's the matter, got a headache?" asked John as he entered the room.

He did not immediately realise that he had just asked a question he did not want to know the answer to. He felt that something serious had happened.

"Sit down, old man," Jacky replied.

John complied, dreading what he was about to be told, but this time praying with all his might that his instincts would fail him.

"I don't know how else to tell you," Jacky continued. "It's Archi. A bomb exploded in the shuttle bay and..." Jacky hesitated, but finally finished with a trembling voice:"I want to tell you that Archi is... dead."

John took the blow and held his head in his hands. A heavy atmosphere hung over the room. Only the hum of the fans cooling the computers broke the silence. After several seconds of heavy quiet, John stood up, looking determined, and let out a loud, bestial scream that shattered the stillness. He seemed relieved for a moment, but the muscles in his face betrayed his distress.

"That bastard Bronski had us bugged," John continued, his eyes moist. "He booby-trapped the hangars and looked me straight in the eye without flinching. Let me get this straight," he continued, his voice drunk with pain and anger. "Out of respect for Archi, we're going to put a stop to this bastard. Then, and only then, will we take the time to mourn him. Do I make myself clear?" he added, staring intently at his comrades.

They all looked at John and nodded in agreement.

"What did Bronski say to you in your apartment?" asked Bedford.

"Not much we don't already know," John replied. "But two very important things. Bronski is untouchable right now. He's built a seemingly impenetrable force field, and we've only got about half an hour to figure it out and save 80% of humanity."

"We didn't know about the force field, but we did know about the countdown," Jacky noted, displaying the contents of the computer on the main wall in front of him.

The counter now displayed in front of their eyes read:

0 h 31 min 27 s

"Bedford and I didn't waste any time while you tried to reason with Bronski. I managed to regain control of some of the computers, but it would take me at least another hour to regain control of the station."

"Then we've lost," Victoria said with a shrug. "I can't believe this murderer will get away with it!"

"Maybe not," Bedford said. "If we can't prevent the capacitors from overloading, there's still a chance we can stop the effects, but it's a dangerous proposition."

"I'm prepared to do whatever it takes to thwart Bronski's plans," John agreed.

"Good timing, if I do say so myself," Jacky continued.

John raised his eyebrows, waiting to hear what Jacky had in store. Knowing his friend's strange sense of humour, he expected the worst.

"Let me explain," Jacky continued. "We all agree that there's nothing we can do to stop Bronski from leaving the station. That leaves us with only one option."

"Do you want to intervene from the ground?" asked Victoria.

"No, if the energy flow reaches the surface, the Earth is lost."

"Then we'll have to intervene from space," Victoria interrupted again.

"Not anymore," said Jacky, annoyed at not being able to finish his sentences. "There are far too many solar panels involved to act in less than half an hour."

Victoria fell silent, and everyone waited feverishly for Jacky to explain his idea.

"Our only option," Jacky continued, "is to intervene. We have to sever Little California's one-legged module to prevent the energy flow from reaching the Earth's crust."

"But the consequences for Stargraber will be disastrous. The one-legged modules aren't just for transporting passengers and power. They're a stabiliser that stiffens the station's structure," Bedford worried.

"That's true," Jacky continued, "but I've done some calculations, and if we create a controlled explosion of sufficient power, we can avoid the worst."

"Allow me to cut you off," Victoria said. "But if you release that much energy into the atmosphere by cutting the one-legged module, the environmental consequences will still be very significant."

"That's why I talked about a controlled explosion, and that's the beauty of my plan. If the blast we're about to create is directed into space, then it is."

"Excuse me for interjecting again," Victoria cut in. "But in order to reach space, doesn't this energy flow have to go through where we are?"

"That's absolutely right, and that's a good thing," Jacky continued, looking at his comrades with conviction. "In a normal explosion, the severed one-legged module will collapse to the ground under the effect of weightlessness, taking all the Stargraber sections with it one by one.

"But thanks to a controlled detonation, the blast will travel up the one-legged module to counteract the downward energy flow created by the capacitor overload. The resulting explosion will destroy the section we're standing on, but the remaining energy will be pushed back into space. This will have the effect of minimising the impact on the rest of the station, as the one-legged module will avoid the domino effect and only take itself down with it."

"That's a good plan," said John, "but how are you going to do it? Let me remind you that all the shuttles have been destroyed, and the elevators are still controlled by Bronski."

"That's where your military training comes in," Jacky replied with a hint of a smile.

John, on the other hand, wasn't smiling at all, waiting to hear what crazy new idea had popped into his friend's head.

"I've turned the problem upside down; the only way to solve it is to jump!"

"I beg your pardon? Pardon? What did he say?" his companions asked in unison.

"You've understood me perfectly, and the only one capable of this feat is you, John."

"But this is madness," Victoria insisted. "You know how high we are. He'll kill himself."

"We're orbiting about 25 miles above the Earth. It's a difficult jump, one you don't see every day, but it's been done before—and John is the only one with the training to do it."

"I've done several jumps up to 9 miles, but we're talking more than twice that," said John. "Aside from the altitude challenge, I don't have the right equipment, and jumping without a pressure suit is out of the question."

"I think I can solve that problem," said Bedford. "We have spacewalking training suits in the gym. They're pressurised and fully functional. The only drawback is that they're stiffer than real space suits."

"It could work," John said with a twinkle in his eye. "Does anyone have any other ideas?" he asked casually.

"Obviously not," Victoria observed. "I still think it's madness."

"Maybe, but I don't have a choice," John replied. "Do you realise what's at stake? We're talking about billions of people. On the other hand, I have to do this in memory of Archi, who wouldn't have allowed any part of what he developed to be used as a weapon of mass destruction."

John had moved closer to Victoria to reassure her, and she had done the same to encourage him.

"As far as I'm concerned, I'm in," John said. "There are only two problems left: Bronski, and installing the explosives on the one-legged module."

"The Bronski problem will take care of itself," said Jacky. "He has blind faith in his force field, and that's what's going to be his downfall. I don't think we should do anything. The energy reflux that will destroy this section will take care of him for us. By the time he realises his mistake, it will be too late."

"As for planting the explosives," Bedford continued, "I'm going to equip you with a pneumatic grappling hook to which we'll attach the explosives. All you have to do is pull the trigger at the right moment to send the explosive into the heart of the one-legged module."

"If we agree with this plan, we'll have to go now," Jacky added, pointing to the countdown, which now read:

0 h 22 min 10 sec.

"It takes more than ten minutes to put on an astronaut suit. With the time it takes to get to the gym, we have to leave now, or we'll miss the jump window. You have to admit, with such a good plan, that would be a shame."

Jacky's sense of humour hadn't quite hit the mark this time, but they were all determined to see this unlikely plan through. Before Jacky had time to finish his sentence, they had already followed John's lead.

Arriving at the gym, Victoria stood back, feeling a little alienated from the proceedings. The others all had specific tasks to complete. John had to put on his pressure suit, Bedford was in charge of the grappling hook and the explosives, and Jacky always had his nose in the computer, calculating the parameters of the free fall.

John's suit had been removed from its place. Its weight of 35 kilos made it unwieldy outside the vacuum of space. Before settling in, John looked around as if to take in the moment. He spotted

Victoria in the background, watching in religious silence as his friends made their preparations.

"Victoria, you can help me," John called across the room.

"I don't know if I should," she said, moving closer to the suit. "For a moment, I felt a little useless. No one cares what I say."

Hearing these words, John moved to stand between Victoria and the suit.

"It's no use," he repeated, "I think just the opposite, Vicky. If you hadn't been here with me, I don't think I would have had the willpower to go through with this plan. Without you by my side, and with Archi's death to deal with, I honestly think I would have hesitated – but not anymore."

Victoria knew that John wouldn't give up and that he needed support.

"Be careful. My presence alone won't protect you from all dangers," she said, trying to lighten the mood.

"I'll do my best," he said, putting his arms around her. "There is so much I would like to say to you since we met, but events have not left us much time to express ourselves."

"Say no more," Victoria interrupted, kissing John on the lips as if she'd never see him again.

Their fiery kiss caught Jacky's attention, and to justify his next move, he once again posted the countdown on the gym's largest wall.

"Ahem." Jacky tried to be as discreet as possible.

Victoria and John seemed to have completely forgotten why they were in the room. Jacky decided to intervene more forcefully. He activated the winch that supported the suit, and in an uncontrolled spin, the arm of the spacesuit came to touch Victoria's buttocks. She jumped instantly, putting an end to the sultry kiss between the two lovebirds.

"Sorry to stop you," Jacky said dryly, "but the clock is ticking," he added, pointing to the countdown, which now read 0 h 16 min 5 sec.

John took another look at the suit, which had a gaping opening in the back to make it easier to put on. Despite all these tweaks, it still took a good ten minutes to get the suit on and adjusted. The counter now read 0 h 5 min 54 sec.

"I'm done," Bedford exclaimed. "I thought I wouldn't make it in time. All I have to do now is attach the grappling hook to your arm. I've attached an explosive halfway between shattering and blasting. I needed a powerful explosion to perforate the one-legged module, and a relatively slow one to control its direction..."

"Sorry to interrupt such an interesting conversation," Jacky cut in, "but we're running out of time and need to get to the point."

"How do I fire your shattering device?" asked John.

"You should feel a trigger on the tip of your index finger. When Jacky gives you the signal by radio, all you have to do is press it. Be careful not to tense up too much as you descend. To overcome the relative stiffness of the suit, the device has been set up to be relatively sensitive. Once the explosive has penetrated the one-legged module, it will detonate almost instantaneously. According to my calculations, if your speed exceeds Mach 1, you shouldn't feel the effects of the blast too much."

"Thanks for telling me; I feel much more relaxed," John said.

"There's only a few minutes left," Jacky insisted, pointing again to the wall, which now showed 0 h 4 min 14 sec. "Your freefall should last between 4 and 4.30 minutes, but for our explosion to be fully effective in pushing the energy flow back towards the station, it will have to be triggered at about 12 miles, which is after 2.15 minutes of flight. That may seem like a long time to you, but trust me, it's a very short time to stabilise and activate the grapple launcher. Your suit is equipped with an automatic opening parachute that activates between 3,300 and 2,000 feet, so you don't have to do anything."

"Anything else?" asked John.

"No," said Jacky. "All we have to do now is wish you good luck. As soon as you're airborne, we'll evacuate to a nearby section for safety. I'll be following you on my cell phone."

Bedford, holding the suit's helmet in his hands, walked over to John to outfit him with his ultimate accessory. Victoria held her breath as if she were about to spend the next ten minutes in apnoea.

The counter now read 0 h 2 min 50 sec. John moved with difficulty towards the decompression chamber.

"Testing, testing. Can you hear me?" said Jacky as he closed the airlock door.

"5 out of 5," John replied. A multitude of information was displayed in ATH in John's helmet. He paid little attention.

"If Bronski wasn't lying to you, which I doubt given his smugness," Jacky continued, "you'll have to jump in 35 seconds to synchronise with the start of the energy flow. As for us, we're going to evacuate. Don't worry, we'll be the last ones. If all goes according to plan, there won't be any collateral damage. I've confirmed that Bronski's son is in isolation in the Chinese module, leaving only his father in our section."

Alone in John's quarters, Mathias Bronski kept an eye on his screens. He gloated as he watched each of the ten capacitor gauges relentlessly fill to the critical zone. Two minutes and twenty seconds to go and he would finally witness a new era of his own making. His plan was going as expected. His only regret was that he didn't have an opponent on his level. John Desmond had done nothing to stop him, and this reinforced his belief that humanity was decadent and lacking in spirit, ready to be reborn under his leadership. He smiled.

The outer door was now open. John, accustomed as he was to using the shuttles, was in awe of the spectacle before him. At this altitude, the curvature of the Earth was really pronounced, and the phrase "blue planet" took on its full meaning at the boundaries of the stratosphere. The view from a spacesuit was even more impressive. He felt almost naked in the immensity of the void.

Jacky's voice in his headset brought him back to reality.

"John, are you ready? Ten more seconds. Remember, if you make it through this, you owe me a favour."

"A favour?" John asked, concentrating hard.

"Yes, the promise you made to get me here," Jacky clarified.

John moved his foot to the edge of the structure.

"In 5, 4, 3, 2, 1, go," Jacky called, making sure he was understood.

John let the weight of the suit pull him down headfirst and began the biggest fall of his life. For the first few seconds, everything seemed to happen in slow motion, in a restful silence. John looked around to make sure he was parallel to the one-legged module. About fifteen seconds had passed when John became aware of the speed at which he was already falling. The one-legged module seemed to fly by as fast as a control tower passes a fighter jet. John estimated his speed at about 185 miles per hour.

The silence was broken by Jacky, who tried to gauge his friend's stress level.

"Are you all right?"

"I'm fine. My speed is picking up," John replied succinctly.

Thirty seconds had passed before John began to feel the effects of speed. His extremities began to tremble slightly, and the trajectory corrections he made with his arms, much like a ski jumper, had little effect. The stability of his entire body was being tested.

After 45 seconds of falling, John tried to estimate his speed again. This time, the surface of the one-legged module seemed to roll like the ground in a low pass. John estimated that he was now falling at over 500 miles per hour. He feared hitting the sound barrier. At over 620 miles per hour, this would inevitably lead to turbulence caused by high aerodynamic pressure and could cause him to lose control of his stability.

A few seconds later, John suddenly lost sight of the one-legged module he'd been using to visualise his trajectory and estimate his speed. His fall now resembled that of a lead-weighted dead leaf spinning on itself, rather than that of an experienced skydiver. He told himself he had just broken the sound barrier, but he didn't hear its characteristic sound—too busy trying to re-establish his trajectory.

His greatest fear was losing consciousness and not being able to activate the grapple launcher in time. All attempts to regain control failed. He decided to let himself go for a while. The tendrils followed each other without pause, beating him like a rag doll.

Doubt began to creep into his mind. Another thirty seconds had passed, and he had only a minute to stabilise himself and launch the explosive at the one-legged module.

"John, you're always with me," said Jacky, his voice echoing in John's head. "Your heart rate is through the roof. Try slowing your breathing, that should help."

"He's not answering," Victoria worried as she stood next to Jacky.

"He probably can't answer at the moment," Bedford reassured her.

Only a few guttural sounds reached them through the speakers.

"Tell him we're safe and sound, I'm sure that'll help."

"John," Jacky continued, in as calm a voice as possible, "we're safe with Victoria, so you can carry out your mission and avenge Archi's death at the same time. Hold on, buddy, I'm with you."

His words gave John a jolt of energy, lifting him out of the black veil that was beginning to appear before his eyes. A few more seconds and he would probably have lost consciousness. He had only 20 seconds left to stabilise himself and adjust his aim to complete his mission. He threw all his remaining strength into the fight.

For a moment, he managed to regain a partially correct trajectory, but he was still not stable enough to aim confidently at the one-legged module.

"How much longer?" he called into his microphone.

Victoria breathed a sigh of relief at the sound of John's voice.

"Another 15 seconds," Jacky replied immediately.

"He's fine, that's wonderful," Victoria added for Jacky's benefit.

Although the seconds ticked away quickly, they still seemed like minutes. He wasn't sure if he was getting used to the situation or if he had slowed down, but he felt that he finally had some control over his movements.

He decided to try a turn, to be able to aim the grapple launcher more calmly. It was his last chance. Miraculously, everything worked as he had imagined. Now, in freefall on his back, he could point his arm at the one-legged module and wait for his friend's final count.

"Eight, seven, six," Jacky said.

Victoria and Bedford's eyes met. But they were unable to say a word, so nervous were they.

"Five, four, three," Jacky continued.

John tweaked the trigger on the tip of his index finger as gently as possible to make sure it was still in place.

"Two, one, zero. Now, John, throw the grappling hook," Jacky called out, sweat on his forehead.

John did so and saw the grappling hook hurtling towards the one-legged module. The speed of the grappling hook was so great, even though the flip had slowed his fall considerably, that he couldn't be sure it had hit its target.

In the next instant, he saw a huge explosion that literally split the one-legged module in two. A gigantic fireball, accompanied by a multitude of metal fragments, lit up the sky. Severed in the middle by the explosion, the one-legged module was now split in two. The enormous fireball began its ascent along the upper part, disintegrating every last remnant of the one-legged module as it went. As for the lower part, it collapsed in on itself like a skyscraper that had been dynamited.

John was relieved. Jacky's plan had worked perfectly. Still, John hadn't expected that the slowdown caused by his toppling would allow the blast of the extraordinary explosion to catch up with him.

Without understanding what was happening to him, a shock as sudden as it was violent made him feel like he was being dismembered. Darkness invaded his brain for good.

"John, can you hear me?" said Jacky. "Hello, John? Answer me, buddy."

All he heard was silence.

"Is he all right?" Bedford asked loudly.

"I don't know. He's not answering," Victoria replied. "I just want to know if he's all right."

"I've got nothing, no answer," Jacky continued, clearly embarrassed, "but we'll know in a few seconds if he saved Earth."

In the evacuated section of Stargraber, only one man remained in John's apartment. Bronski was visibly nervous. In a matter of seconds, the flow of life-saving energy would descend upon the

Earth, explode Yellowstone, and propel him as the new saviour of mankind.

In fact, he would be the first to realise that John had succeeded in his mission. Without understanding why, he had just lost all contact with the sensors installed along the one-legged module that allowed him to track the progress of his Machiavellian plan. It took him some time to realise what had caused the loss of most of his connections.

When he finally understood, his face changed. A strong, growing vibration told him that a major problem was about to jeopardise his plan. One by one, his screens began to show nothing but static. He decided to focus his attention on the only monitors that were still working.

As he looked at the cameras he had placed under the roof and outside the arrival hall of the one-legged module, the surprise on his face instantly changed to an expression of horror. Before his eyes, the one-legged module was collapsing at the speed of a galloping horse. He then realised that the vibrations he felt were the precursors of a more violent shock, probably caused by an explosion whose blast travelled the length of the one-legged module.

He hadn't expected such a thing to happen, and he knew that the direct result would be the destruction of the section he was in within seconds. He knew that the explosion would end its course in space. Earth would suffer little damage. His plan was destroyed. All was lost. He had lost.

How could this be? How could he be so wrong?

He withdrew his hands from the keyboard in front of him and bowed his head, resigned to the end.

Epilogue

Victoria, Bedford and Jacky walked solemnly into the New Albuquerque Mortuary Medical Centre.

"Victoria, did you remember the flowers?" said Jacky, breaking the heavy silence. "We owe him that much, at least."

"I took care of them," Victoria replied. "I had them sent over this morning."

"Considering the number of people who came to pay their respects, he must be covered in them," Bedford added.

"John sacrificed himself to save us. We could have thought of something more elaborate than a few flowers. We should be ashamed of ourselves," Victoria snapped.

"I admire what he did, but when Bedford and I heard the news this morning, it was the first thing that came to mind under the circumstances," Jacky said. "After coming here the last few days and seeing him inactive, we didn't know what else to do. We felt a little helpless."

"However," Bedford continued, "it was a relief to know that this was the last time we would have to go to this morbid place to see him."

The three friends went straight to the centre's front desk to find out if John had been moved. They made their way up the stairs to the second floor, through the long ICU corridor, and finally to John's room. Victoria, leading the way, hesitated for a moment before entering. She was suddenly overcome with emotion. Nevertheless, she entered first, followed by her two companions.

John lay there with his arms at his sides.

"He looks fine," Jacky whispered.

"Yes," Victoria confirmed in the same tone.

She moved closer and kissed him on the forehead. She couldn't hold back a few tears that ran down her cheek and landed on John's face.

"I hope they're tears of joy," John stammered, his eyes half open.

John grabbed the remote from his bed to help him sit up.

"Good to see you again, John," Bedford said.

"You didn't lie to us," Jacky laughed. "He's regained consciousness and doesn't seem to have any residual effects. It's a shame in a way, but you gave us quite a scare, mate. We thought you were never going to wake up."

"Too bad," John wondered?

"Well, yes," said Jacky. "For a moment, I thought I might have an opening with Vicky, you know."

Victoria reflexively poked Jacky in the shoulder to make it clear that his gravelly sense of humour had its limits.

"Thank you all for being here," John said, his voice still weak. "If I'm in bed, I guess we won?"

"You guess right, my friend," Jacky replied. "The explosion was enormous, carrying our entire Stargraber section into space without damaging the rest of the station. A masterpiece. Now you can keep your promise."

"Sorry," John replied. "I don't remember. Probably the fall," he added, pointing to his head.

"Will you tell us what John promised you, instead of beating around the bush?" Victoria asked.

"John said that if I helped him with Stargraber, he'd give me his little red notebook for free."

John suddenly turned the colour of his supposed notebook.

"May I ask what's in it?" asked an intrigued Victoria, who had noticed John's embarrassment.

"It's a simple list that belongs in the past," John replied, looking tenderly at Victoria.

"The past?" Jacky raised his voice. "On the contrary, it's my future. It's a list of the names of all the girls we met during our army training. I was too young then to realise that these notes would become so important over the years. It's the greatest gift of all."

"You'll get it; what's said is said... Any news of Bronski?" asked John, trying to change the subject.

Victoria couldn't help smiling. *Another point I'll be sure to bring up when we're alone,* she thought.

"I'm afraid he left with the rest of the train," Bedford replied. "No one could have escaped that hellhole."

"Right now, he's somewhere between us and Venus," Jacky added.

For once, everyone laughed at Jacky's joke. John choked slightly and put his hand in Victoria's as she sat on the edge of his bed. Bedford and Jacky realised their friends needed to be alone together.

"We'll leave you to it," Jacky said as he headed for the door. "We'll see you when you get out. Have a good rest."

Victoria and John were finally alone.

"Were you scared?" asked John.

"That's a funny question," she replied. "Of course I was terribly worried."

"That's all right," he told her with a charming smile. "I just wanted to find out how much you'd miss me."

"Enormously," she said, sinking her green eyes into his. "Enormously..."

The End